The Sailor's Return

The Sailor's Return

David Garnett

MINT EDITIONS

The Sailor's Return was first published in 1925.

This edition published by Mint Editions 2021.

ISBN: 9781513299631 | E-ISBN: 9781513223773

Published by Mint Editions®

minteditionbooks.com

Publishing Director: Jennifer Newens
Design & Production: Rachel Lopez Metzger
Project Manager: Micaela Clark
Typesetting: Westchester Publishing Services

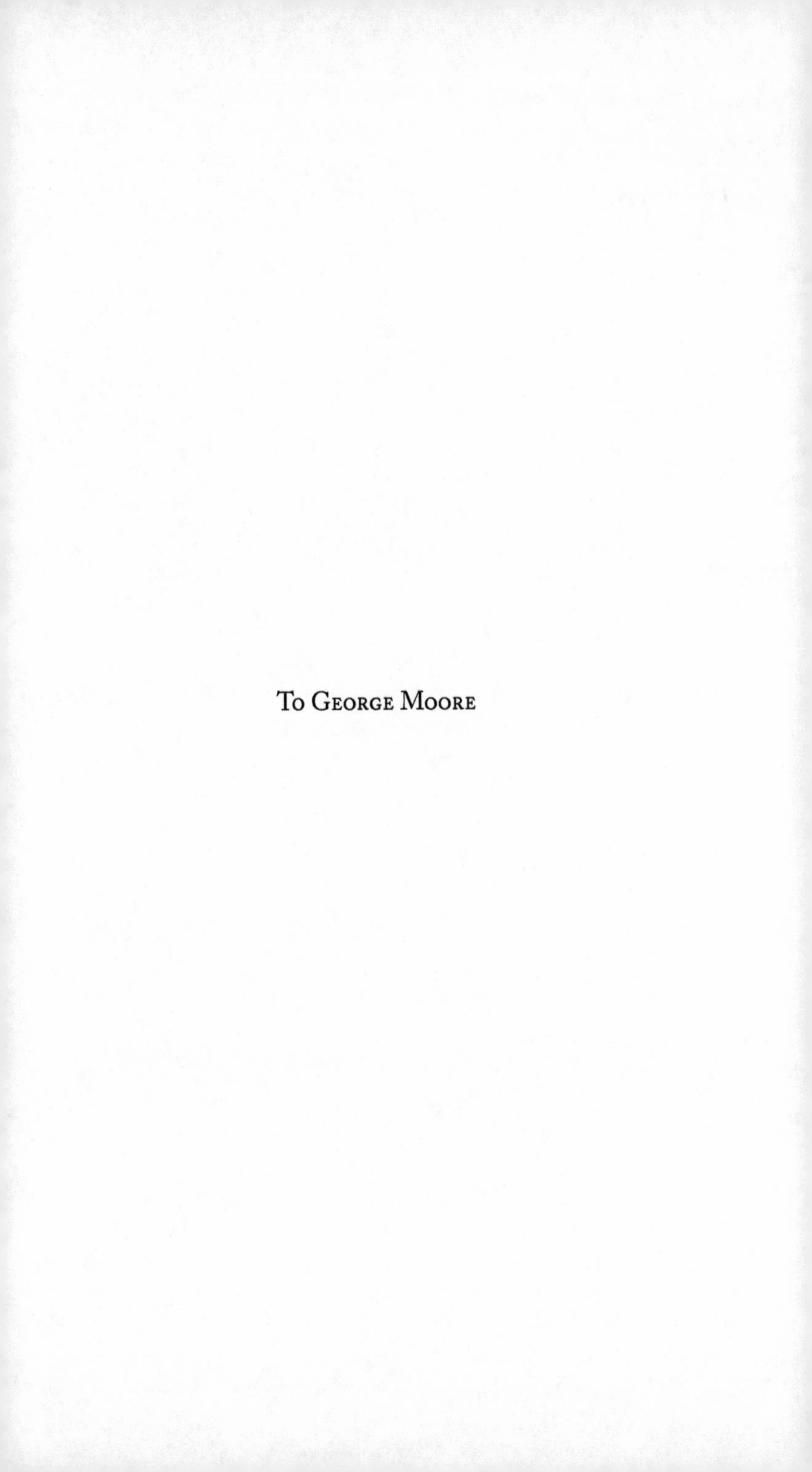

To George Moore

Perfection is in unity; prefer
One woman first, and then one thing in her.

—DONNE

The *Duke of Kent* came safe into Southampton Docks on the tenth of June, 1858.

On board of her was a mariner named William Targett, returning to his own country as a passenger, having shipped at Lisbon. He was in no hurry to go ashore, and waited half an hour for the confusion to be straightened out on board, and the turmoil to subside on land, before he motioned to the young negro who accompanied him to bear a hand with a large basket of woven grass. They carried it down the gangway between them and deposited it on the side of the dock.

"Stand there Tulip, till I come back," said the sailor, who then went on board once more to return carrying a small sea chest on his shoulder and a wicker cage containing a parrot in his hand. Targett was a strongly made man, a trifle over six feet in height, with thick dun-coloured hair bleached by the tropic sun which had tanned his skin a darker colour. He carried himself with an air of independence, or rather with that air of authority which comes with the habit of command. Beside this Hercules the African seemed a child, whose black and curly head scarcely reached to the seaman's shoulder. The most noticeable thing about Tulip was an ebony black skin, without a touch of brown or of grey. In figure the negro was fragile, he held himself straight as an arrow. His savage bones were small and delicate; one might have fancied them light as a bird's, and like a bird's bones filled with air. The features were regular; the nose short, but straight and thick, and as powerful as a tomcat's; the nostrils and lips spreading like those of a child pressed against the panes of a village sweetshop; but the mouth itself was small, and the teeth were fine, regular and white as sugar.

Both Targett and his companion were dressed in new, but rough and coarsely made clothes, bought at a marine store in Lisbon, but the negro, whose thick gold ear-rings betrayed his vanity, had wound a scarlet handkerchief round his throat, and his striking appearance soon attracted the attention of all the sailors and loafers at the docks. At another moment he would have been accosted by several, but the business of unloading the newly-arrived vessel prevented anything more than passing salutes and jocular cries, to which the darkey made no response beyond a proud toss of the head. Targett's return put an end to these attentions. Once clear of the docks, the sailor hailed a four-wheeler and drove to the "Dolphin," one of the best houses in the centre of the town. There he engaged a room, and ordered hot dinner to be brought up for him and the young negro.

In the evening he went out to a money-changer's, and afterwards to a jeweller's. Ten minutes later he returned whistling to the Dolphin. Next morning saw him with his negro, parrot, basket and sea chest at Southampton railway station. He took tickets for Poole, and bundled his possessions into an empty carriage. As they were starting, a horsey-looking man got in with them. They travelled in silence, until the stranger, who had been staring at Targett for half an hour, spoke:

"Reckon you've been abroad?"

Targett nodded. Then he glanced at Tulip, and at each of his possessions in turn, smiled and said: "So you might guess, Sir, from my having a parrot with me."

"Can he speak?" asked the horsey-looking man.

"Not extraordinary," answered the sailor, "but sometimes you could swear it was a baby crying."

"I've a family of seven of my own, thank you," said the horsey-looking man, "without parrots."

"I don't know where he learnt the trick," said Targett, "unless he was once in a large family like yours, but he has learnt it, and it's just like a young child, strike me if it ain't."

"Feathered bipeds they call those birds for being so human," said the stranger.

The line ran through Ringwood. There the horsey-looking man got out on his way to the stables at Stockbridge, and there pointing out of the window, the sailor spoke for the first time to his companion.

"This is my county. It begins here."

The blackamoor did not answer, he only looked at Targett with a worshipping face, and then turned again to the landscape of Dorset, and then back again to the sailor.

Next moment he was once more looking out of the window. His expression was alert and watchful. He started with every creak of the railway carriage; he listened to the grinding of the wheels and the puffing of the engine; and at every bump and jar of the slow train on the uneven track he glanced with apprehension at the basket, which lay beside him on the seat of the carriage, and on which one of his lean hands rested.

Now that they were alone in the carriage, Targett watched the negro silently for some moments, and a pitying smile came over his face.

"Now then, Tulip," he said, "take it easy. The train will do you no mischief."

The negro looked at his master in a shamefaced way, at once humble and contrite, but the next minute he quivered like a greyhound as the train passed over a culvert, and again he clutched at the basket.

"You can take Sambo out if you like," said the sailor.

Tulip at once undid the catch of the basket, which was a very neatly made affair, pierced with a dozen small holes and ornamented with a pattern of dyed grasses, red and green, and with handles at each end.

A little boy, between two and three years of age, in colour the duskiest shade of brown, was revealed lying upon his back, with his eyes open, diligently sucking the first two fingers of his left hand. For a moment or two the young stowaway lay motionless, seeming to be dazzled by the light of day, but presently he sat up, took his paw out of his mouth, and began to address Tulip in a childish jargon, interrupting his odd words with peals of merry laughter, shouts and gurgles. Tulip picked him up out of his basket, or covered cradle, and fondled him very lovingly, but presently set him down on the floor of the carriage, so that he could trot about. Young Sambo was rather small for his age, but perfectly well made and very muscular, and he looked about him with an air of calm inquiry and intelligence, noting the motion of the train, the structure of the carriage, with its doors and windows, and he ran across very soon to look out first on one side and then on the other. In all this there was a total absence of fear, or of dismay, at finding himself in strange surroundings, very remarkable in a young child. Targett watched the little boy with an approving smile, and took him onto his knee, and in that way they travelled the rest of the way to Poole, with the sailor pointing out to Sambo all the horses and cows in the fields which they could see from out of the window.

When they arrived at Poole, Sambo was not put back into his basket, Targett telling the negro to carry the little boy and leave the luggage for a porter. The sailor then led the way to the Swan Inn and asked for a bedroom.

The innkeeper's wife looked at him inquisitively.

"Whatever's that?" she asked, peering past his elbow at Tulip in the passage.

"My mate has a baby there; the rest of the things are being brought along by a porter."

"A baby! You don't mean it!" exclaimed Mrs. Cherrett, the hostess of the Swan, and she pushed by Targett to see for herself.

"Why, it's black," she exclaimed in a tone of horror. "Poor little chap—he's as black as his father. How dreadful! I didn't think they would have got so black at that age."

Sambo stared back at Mrs. Cherrett with perfect self-possession, while she fussed over him like a hen clucking over an egg. Her noise indeed had much the same effect, for all the women in the house came running into the passage until there were six or seven of them collected round Tulip. Soon they began to poke the little boy with their fingers and even to try and take him from the negro's arms, while Sambo, with widely open eyes, glanced first questioningly, and then appealingly at his protector.

"That's enough now," said Targett. "That child is in the proper hands; show me up now to my room."

"Don't let that nasty man keep him! Proper hands indeed! What can a man expect to know about children? We'll take the little boy down to the kitchen and look after him," cried one of the maids, and the cook actually laid her cheek against Sambo's sooty hide.

At this the barmaid gave a scream. "How can you Mrs. Bascombe? Why, I wouldn't touch the creature for the world!"

"Come on now," said Targett, "show us upstairs."

"Poor little shrimp!" said Mrs. Cherrett, "This way, Sir. Maggie, you run and bring up some milk for the little boy."

"Or some potatoes and gravy, if you have got them," said Targett.

"I've never seen such a thing in my life," said the barmaid. "A sailorman coming back to England with a little blackamoor! I've known them bring parrots and monkeys often enough, but not children. Just like a black imp from hell too, but there's no knowing what won't take their fancy."

"So there's still hope for you, Annie. The sailorman might take you on his next voyage to Africa and you would be as fine a curiosity there as the nigger boy is here," said the cook.

"You saucebox!" said Annie indignantly, and flounced into the bar. But she put her head back and said: "you had better take the blackamoor's father into the kitchen, Mrs. Bascombe. If you ask him nicely he'll make you a present of a black baby." Then recollecting that she ought always to be quite ladylike, she mopped an imaginary tear from her eye, tidied her hair and took a sip of gin and afterwards a second sip to calm her feelings and prepare herself for the next young farmer who stepped into the private bar.

The following day Targett and his Tulip went out shopping in the morning (after carefully locking the little boy up in their room so that the chambermaid could not get at him).

When they had walked up and down both sides of Market Street and High Street, William Targett came at last to a decision, and taking Tulip by the hand entered the shop of Mrs. Frickes, Modiste.

"I want you to rig this lady with the best dresses you have got; for she is a lady. She is wearing these clothes because she has only just come ashore, and now she wants the best of everything that money can buy. Don't be afraid, I can pay for all." This was a strange speech, but William uttered it slowly and deliberately, addressing himself to Mrs. Frickes in person.

That good woman stared very hard, but soon pulled out boxes of dresses, for she never lost custom if she could help it.

Tulip remained unmoved until Targett said he would look back in an hour's time. Then she took firm hold of his hand and said:

"Please stay to choose the dresses. I shall be afraid without you."

Targett frowned, pulled his hand away and swung his arms, but he stayed in the shop after all, and Mrs. Frickes had to bring out all the readymade dress models of the latest fashions which she had, and a dozen or two rolls of material.

One of the models was chosen for the good reason that it was the only one which fitted. It was a cream silk, with red and golden butterflies and flowers worked upon it, short sleeves, trimmed with real Irish lace, and a ruffler of the same lace at the neck. Besides this dress, two workaday gowns were ordered to be made. Having bought the dresses, Targett remembered underclothes, and a crinoline, which had to be got at the draper's next door. Mrs. Frickes very kindly came with the couple to Mr. Catt's. And there Targett was at liberty to stand looking out of the window after he had said:

"A dozen pair of stockings, a dozen of handkerchiefs, and six of everything else."

Only once was he appealed to—on the subject of stays.

"We'll take a pair for luck," he decided, "but she need not wear them now."

Mr. Catt was sufficiently obliging to put a room at her disposal where Tulip could change her clothes. While she was dressing, Targett remembered shoes and sent round for a shoemaker to come to Mr. Catt's.

At last Tulip was clothed, stockinged, and shod, the bills were paid, and they were ready to depart.

But the news that a negro had turned out to be a woman in disguise had already begun to spread through the town, and as they came out of Mr. Catt's shop a dozen or more people were waiting to see her. A gasp of surprise, even of admiration, was heard on all sides, for Tulip was very finely dressed now and looked quite a grand lady in her new clothes, though to be sure her poor face was still black.

But she was so childishly happy, so innocently delighted, and gave the crowd such sweet smilwith an air of independees that any hostility they may have felt before was instantly dispelled. Nothing but wonder and pleasure at having seen such a sight remained in the minds of the onlookers.

Later in the day clothes were bought for the little boy Sambo, and when they took the train that evening he was no longer hidden in the basket, but made to sit on his mamma's knee and then on his papa's all the way to Dorchester. For that, of course, was the relationship of Targett, Tulip, and the black baby.

In his basket young Sambo had known how to lie quiet so that few people on the passage from Lisbon had suspected the child's existence. He had been brought up in the strict discipline of young negroes, who are famous for an intelligence and self-control never seen at two years old in our white children. The little blacks acquire this precocity from the conditions of danger and hardship in which they live, for at any moment in Africa a leopard may slink into the village, an alligator crawl out of the nearest pond, a poisonous serpent rear itself up under the first tottering footsteps of a child. Such dangers are almost beyond our imagination; lions, leopards, rhinoceroses, and gigantic riverhorses, snakes, baboons, gorillas, and a thousand kinds of wild beasts infest the continent. The village may be stampeded by elephants drawn up in line like Nelson's fleet at the action of Trafalgar, each fifty yards from his towering tusky fellow, or it may be slowly sapped away by ants moving blindly over the earth in armies vaster than those which spread over Europe in the year eighteen hundred and twelve.

Indeed, it is not to be wondered at that the smallest children should be obedient coming from such a land where there is no need of parents calling up bogeys, like the Great Agrippa, to terrify them. The chief difficulty that Targett and his Tulip found on shipboard was in keeping the child clean, and in giving him exercise. He was of an age when he was able to eat any ordinary food, and indeed subsisted for the four days between Lisbon and Southampton on ship's biscuit soaked in gravy. Exercise was the difficulty, and after once or twice nearly having him discovered, his parents were forced to deny it him, for Targett had a particular reason for keeping the child hid. To be sure his black skin rendered him nearly invisible in the dark, and sometimes his father would give him an airing at night. Otherwise he had to keep to his basket, to lie still and keep from making the slightest sound when strangers were by.

It was a great treat to Sambo and to his mother also now that this journey was over, for though it had not lasted more than six days it seemed to them as if it had been as many months.

In Dorchester their arrival made quite a stir, so much so indeed that wherever they went in the old town they found it wearing a holiday look, because so many people bustled out of the shops to see them, loitered along the same street, or stopped in the road and stared at them frankly, and turned round to gape again until they were out of sight.

It was this that made Tulip tell Targett that Dorchester was a very much finer town than Poole. For the black girl liked the bustle as much as some English ladies would have disliked it, and that although she saw that it was largely because of herself and her child.

They had greeted Targett in her country with as much excitement as was now displayed on her arrival in England. They had made no bones about staring at him in Dahomey.

This remark of Tulip's set William at his ease, and without worrying about those who chose to stare, he made his way along the High Street till he came to Mrs. Gulliver's beer-house, where he asked for a room, and there they stayed the night. The next day Targett employed himself in visiting a tailor's, and in spying out the land, since he had business in Dorchester which demanded a certain amount of circumspection and inquiry.

This was no more nor less than the changing of the whole course of his life. Till that time he had been nothing but a mariner, having followed the sea for some fourteen years, ever since he was a boy of sixteen. Now he had decided to retire from his profession and become a publican. He had to inquire into the hundred details appertaining to the business he proposed to adopt, as well as the general state of the trade itself and the opportunities it afforded in that part of England.

The best thing he could do to find out this was to take his pipe and spend the day in the different bars and parlours of the Dorchester taverns. Thus Targett spent three days, drinking first with the landlord of one house and then with him of another. It was not hard after speaking of his life as a sailor and of the wonderful places that he had seen in the East, to turn and say: "You fellows have the best of it ashore! Damme if I don't envy you your trade! Though I daresay you think that I should just broach a keg of rum and set to, and you wouldn't hear anymore of me for a week."

In the course of these conversations, and for the price of half a gallon of gin, Targett found out a great deal about the trade.

Tulip meanwhile spent most of her time indoors, in her room at Mrs. Gulliver's, looking after her little boy. Once a day she took him out for a walk, but the crowd of people that followed them sometimes became an embarrassment to her, particularly the children, who pressed about her legs, and were not happy unless they could touch, pat, or pinch little Sambo.

Soon the word went round that the big stranger had left the sea in order to become a showman, and that Tulip and her baby and the parrot, were the advance guard of his collection. Lions, hyænas and other wild beasts were said to be on their way to Dorchester. This story, like many another of the same sort, never came to the ears of the man about whom it was told.

After a day's idleness, to let the fumes of rumpunch and gin and water get out of his head, Targett put on his new suit of navy serge, took his stick of ivory, and called at the office of Wm. Estrich and Pardon, Brewers.

Old Mr. Estrich kept his visitor waiting twenty minutes and then came out of his office to inspect him. "What's your name and what's your business with me, Sir?" he asked.

"My name is Targett, William Targett. I hold a master's certificate from Trinity House, but have no longer a command. Now I am leaving the sea and want to set up in the licensed trade, so I have come to you, thinking you can help me."

"Help you—what, with money? You are mistaken there!" said Mr. Estrich, looking hard at Targett.

"No, Sir—I have plenty of that; help me to find a good house."

"Come in to my office and sit down, Mr. Targett," said old Estrich.

When they were seated he continued: "If you must go into the licensed trade you must, and it is no business of mine to dissuade you. But the life of an innkeeper is not the life for everybody, and in particular it is not the life for a retired seaman. It is my experience of sailors that they drink hard, and while the bout is on they don't care if everything goes to the devil. Now an innkeeper must always be sober enough to attend to his business, or if he isn't sober he must appear so. That's the reason why gentlemen's servants make good innkeepers—they are such damned hypocrites and toadies. No! If you're a seaman you had better go back to sea again. The land is no place for you."

Targett reached for his hat and stick and got up to go.

"Don't run off like that; good gracious me!" cried old Mr. Estrich, and then banging a bell on his desk, he shouted: "Boy! Hi—there, boy! Bring the tantalus and some clean glasses."

"If you bar seamen it is no good my wasting your time or mine any longer," said Targett still standing.

"Sit down, Mr. Targett, sit down. If you must have a house you must. I was just warning you, but nobody likes good advice; that's only natural. My father would have sent me into the Navy when I was twelve years old, but I begged and prayed to stop at home and my mother was on my side. I have never ceased to regret it. That is by the way; but what sort of house do you want?"

"It must be a good house, and the only house in the village. I don't want any bad blood with another man," said Targett.

"I haven't a house vacant anywhere. But how much money have you got?"

"I'm not sure yet," said Targett, "how much it amounts to, but there is plenty and to spare to rent such a house, or even to buy it if it were a small place."

"No, there are no licensed houses in the market; you can put that idea out of your head," said Mr. Estrich, "I'm sorry we have nothing. Wasn't young Stingo in here yesterday?" he shouted through the door. "Didn't he say something about wanting a tenant for 'The Sailor's Return' at Maiden Newbarrow?"

A voice came from the room beyond, but Targett could not distinguish the words.

"Well, he told me he did," said Mr. Estrich. "Now then, Mr. Targett, I shall give you a letter for young Stingo who wants a tenant, and you may suit each other. But mind you don't pay him more than thirty pounds a year in rent, and never get into his debt. Never get into debt at all, but least of all to your brewer."

After leaving Mr. Estrich, Targett went round to his acquaintances in the bars of Dorchester and stood them a number of drinks so as to find out the reputation that the Maiden Newbarrow public-house had in the trade. That afternoon he went to Mr. Stingo's office and signed the lease for "The Sailor's Return" without even having visited the village.

Two days later Targett with Tulip and Sambo set off for Maiden Newbarrow, mounted upon a large waggon loaded with furniture which had been bought hastily in Dorchester.

They started early in the morning and had gone some miles when the sun rose. Their way lay along bye roads which led through rolling country towards the sea. The sun shone, the grass sparkled with dew, in the hedges there were bushes of faintly blushing dogrose in full blossom. Tulip, perched high above the chestnut carthorse in the shafts, began singing. Presently she fell silent and the seaman began a loud and rolling chanty. There was no one on the road that morning to hear them singing, or to watch them pass by.

Goldfinches flew out of the hedges, yellowhammers sped from bush to bush in front of them. A cuckoo late in changing his tune mocked as he flew from tree to tree. They passed through two villages and stopped in each of them long enough for the carter to get a can of beer and drink it.

At midday they entered a green valley which led through the downs to the sea. The road was enclosed by stone walls and bordered by occasional ash trees. A mile further on the walls fell away and at the ends of the fields gates barred their progress.

Both Tulip and the sailor were silent as they drew round a corner into view of a small village.

There was an open green with high and mighty sycamores, and underneath them scattered groups of thatched cottages, with white walls.

Geese, grazing by the roadside, lifted their heads and walked away at their approach. A little boy who had been playing knucklebones stood up and stared while they passed.

They turned the corner and saw "The Sailor's Return" before them, standing alone a hundred yards or so from the village. It was a long low house, heavily thatched, with a post standing at one side to take a sign, but the sign had decayed and the frame stood empty.

The shutters were up. On the left-hand side was another green, with a stream beyond. Some ducks embarked in it on seeing them. Across the front of the house was painted: "Stingo's Priory Ales." The painted letters were flaking off.

As they drew up from the village green to the inn several heads appeared over the garden walls, but these were soon withdrawn. One or two women came out of their cottages to look at the waggon, but went indoors again at once as if they had expected to see something else, and were disappointed.

They came to rest in front of the inn, Targett climbed down and took little Sambo from Tulip, who jumped down after him, and began to clap her hands with delight, then picking up Sambo, she danced up to the door. When William had unlocked it they saw before them a bare flagged passage; they smelt an odour of stale beer. There were dead bees on the window-sill, and a spider scuttled into the corner. Targett and Tulip saw these things, but they did not think of them, for this was their home now—they had travelled five thousand miles to find it.

The sailor flung up the shutters, and unfastened a window. On each side of the passage was a bar. Behind was a parlour and a passage leading to the kitchen on one side, and to the dining-room on the other.

The kitchen was large and airy, with whitewashed beams. Beyond it there was a washhouse, a pantry, a scullery, and an outhouse leading to the stables.

Targett however did not look any further.

"Go, make a fire," said he to Tulip, "Undo our hamper. We will bring in a table and chairs by and by, then set the meal, for we shall be hungry when our work's done."

The carter had taken the ropes off the waggon and the two men began to unload the furniture. First came the glasses, which were carried into a safe place. Then all the household goods—beds, bedding, tables, wardrobes, chairs, chests of drawers, and washstands; all were set down on the green in front of the house before being carried indoors.

This was too interesting an event for the villagers of Maiden Newbarrow to pass over altogether, though they were shy of the newcomers, and did not ordinarily permit themselves to display curiosity. As usually is the case in England, they showed their interest in their neighbours rather by surreptitious eavesdropping than by direct observation, or by open questions. However, on this occasion Freddy Leake, the blacksmith, came up to Targett and said:

"I suppose you are our new landlord. I'll lend you a hand moving in. Old Burden can spare me from the forge."

Targett gave him a keen look and shook hands with him, saying as he did so:

"That's right. My name is Targett and I am the landlord. What's yours?"

"Fred Leake, smith's mate."

Other village people began to walk out to the public house in twos and threes. When they reached it they lingered a moment, almost stopped, and then walked on to the one cottage which lay beyond the inn.

Old Mrs. Archer had never before had so many visitors in an evening. Each leant over her fence, pulled a sprig of sweet-smelling marjoram, and said:

"New landlord's moving in, Mrs. Archer. There'll be some beer for harvest."

"I don't know what the men want with all that beer. I am sorry to see them come," said Mrs. Archer. "Better have no neighbours than rowdy ones."

"They say there's a black woman he's brought along with him."

"There," said Mrs. Archer, "what did I tell you? Fine neighbours indeed. But it makes no difference to the men. They'll go anywhere as long as they can get fuddled."

Soon the waggon was unloaded, and the furniture was all carried indoors, but not before there were further offers of assistance. First came the postman, who had a letter for Mr. Targett from London, which had to be signed for and which was sealed with red wax and string. He seemed in no hurry, and took off his coat and worked away with a will. Then came Charley Nye, the rabbit-catcher, who gave advice, although he did not do any work. At last they had finished carrying in all the furniture, and had arranged it in the rooms somehow, and had put up the beds. The carter harnessed his horses, getting ready to go back to Dorchester. The smith and Charley and one or two others who had joined them only waited for his departure to go themselves, when a jingling was heard, and the brewer's big dray came round the corner. The horses were fat and shiny, and moved with that slightly tipsy, dancing gait, which is the sign of all good brewery horses. Perhaps they give them beer in the stables, or feed them on the sprouted grains of barley.

The two men were as large and shiny as the horses, and the dray itself was loaded high with barrels of beer, and here and there a little keg of rum, a small firkin of port wine, a cask of sherry, and a case of spirits.

Such a lot of barrels had not been seen for many years in Maiden Newbarrow. The last tenant of "The Sailor's Return" had been heavily in debt to Mr. Stingo, and at the end his credit had been so utterly exhausted that when he had spent his ready money that should have gone to pay the brewer, he could not buy the beer which was his stock-in-trade. On these occasions the public house was shut up, and then the women laughed and the men grumbled. So this great dray-load of barrels of all sorts and kinds of beer, twopenny, threepenny, and fourpenny, not to speak of foreign wines and spirits, was like the sight of a great treasure ship to the farm labourers. The haymakers had seen it moving along the valley as they worked, from far off on each side of the road. Each one promised himself a happy evening at "The Sailor's Return," for it was many weeks since they had tasted liquor other than the small beer some would brew for themselves. And the sight of those great barrels heaped upon the dray made their dry throats bearable to them, yes—even a pleasure. With each breath that they took of the dry hayseed dust, they promised themselves an extra pint of cool old ale that night.

"We shall have our work cut out to drink them dry," they said to each other as they pointed to the far-off dray, with the bulging barrels heaped upon it, and the fat brown horses flashing their polished brasses in the burning sun.

The great dray drew up, a ladder with crooked rungs of iron was put in position for the barrels to slide down, and then attached to the thickest ropes they were trundled behind the bar or let down into the cellar. Mallets were found to drive the bungs and spigots, and to secure the wooden taps. Glasses were unpacked from the straw crate and rinsed. Soon the first pints of ale were frothing at the lips of the rabbit-catcher, the postman and the smith's mate, and the two draymen.

This sight on the evening of a hot June day overcame the shyness of the villagers. The men marched up in twos and threes and shouted a welcome to the sailor.

The next morning the potman came to the inn. This was a native of the Isle of Wight, whom Targett had engaged in Dorchester. He was a young man, by name Tom Madgwick, of about the middle size, fresh complexioned, with curly hair and a merry disposition (if you would call a man so who was never known to laugh outright). But to make up for this peculiarity he was most of his time smiling and always seemed to have a joke of his own which it was his business to hide away, yet there was nothing supercilious in him; rather he was naturally innocent and civil in his manners, and anxious to please. He was a hard worker too, and Targett could not have found a more honest servant had he searched through the whole kingdom.

Young Tom Madgwick's readiness to work was tested at the moment of his arrival, for there were a thousand jobs to be done that morning in the house. There were floors to be scrubbed, curtain rods to be fixed, carpets to be laid, beds to be pieced together, and all the furniture to be redisposed upon second thoughts about the house, and moved from the rooms to which it had first been taken.

Then again some order was necessary in the arrangement of the bar, shelves had to be put up in new places to accommodate the bottles; in the cellars there were barrels to be lifted onto trestles, and many of these barrels had to be at once broached and tapped. In short there was enough hard work to last two men for nearly a week, and then in addition there was the bar to be minded whenever a carter dropped in for a quart of ale, or a child came over with a jug to carry beer for his father's dinner. Besides all this, Targett had to undertake the whole management of the house, both in keeping his accounts (which he neglected, logging them all it is true, but rarely looking into the book afterwards, or casting up his expenses or reckoning his profits) and also in provisioning the household. Thus at every moment he was called off to see the butcher, the baker or the grocer, or else he had to make out a list of things that must come out from Dorchester, and do this while the carrier's cart was waiting.

This part of his work was that which ordinarily is the business of the innkeeper's wife. Here was an opportunity for Targett to see his mistake in having brought with him a black negro woman from Africa instead of choosing a plain honest stay-at-home woman of his own country. But this reflection never came into the sailor's head, and indeed it was one which all his life he never made. The reason must have been either that he liked this black woman of his so much that he never saw the inconvenience of her, or else that it was his nature never to go back on any mistake once he had made it, or even to admit it to himself.

But it must not be imagined that Tulip was idle. No indeed, she took off the fine clothes that Targett had bought for her at Poole, and wearing nothing but her old sailor's jumper and a petticoat, worked all day, fetching and carrying, polishing the pewter mugs till they shone like silver, and cooking the dinner, though at first she made some laughable mistakes in that art. Then there was her little Sambo whom she had always to be minding lest he should fall into any mischief or danger.

But however hard she might work at the best it was but doing what she was bid, whereas if she had been an Englishwoman she would have managed a whole province of the household, and taken it so completely off her husband's shoulders that he would never need to know that it existed, and might all his life long believe that the beds made themselves each morning and changed their linen every Saturday of their own accord.

But Targett very soon found an occupation in which he could employ Tulip in all her spare time. That was in painting, for he had set to work to repaint all the woodwork of the house, room by room, within a week of moving in.

So poor Tulip was kept sandpapering away the paint, and washing it down afterwards with hot water and soda in readiness for the first coat, then in mixing the paint and laying it on, then cleaning up all the spots of it that chanced to be spilt on the floor.

After a few more days she was given greater time for this job, for Targett found that the kitchen was beyond his management as much as it was beyond hers, and so he hired a woman to come in every morning to get the meals ready and afterwards to wash the dirty plates.

This woman was a body of about sixty, but very active, and strong enough to do a day's work at the wash tub, so that during the week she was two whole days in the house, the first washing and the second ironing.

Her name was Eglantine Clall; she was a widow that had no sons or daughters, nor indeed any relatives living in that neighbourhood. Only a young stonemason lived with her as her lodger. In the village she was rather passed over than spoken of, and had no cronies, so that when there was a wedding or any such junketing she could never take part in it. She made up for this by always attending funerals (which do not require particular invitation from the principal party).

Another man would have lightened his labour, but perhaps heightened the inconvenience, by calling in painters, paperhangers, and a carpenter; but Targett was trained to think that things were best done if he did them himself, and all the work of the renovation of "The Sailor's Return" (for it was nothing else) was done by him, Tulip and their servant Tom.

This was like a true British sailor, who has come to be known all over the world as a "handy-man." There was no piece of work which Targett could not discover the knack of doing. His sea chest held the proof of it, being three parts full of different tools, ranging from a bradawl to a sextant.

As this work proceeded "The Sailor's Return" soon became the very picture of what a country inn should be. It had about it also something brisk and nautical, as much in the style of a crack China clipper as in that of a wayside hostelry.

The parrot's cage hung in the window, and the parrot greeted everyone who passed with a hearty: "Look alive! Look alive! Service! Service!" to which the sailor very soon trained it.

The front of the house had been whitewashed. Above the door was the figurehead from an old frigate, and this had now been repainted and regilded, so that it shone resplendent in the sun. The very curtains of the window were reefed back like the sails of a ship.

With all these improvements, Targett and Tulip were kept so busy that they had very little time to go abroad, or to make any acquaintance in the village. There too it was the busiest moment of the year. The spring had been a late one, and harvest followed quickly upon haymaking; all the labourers were kept working till after dark; the women went out into the fields, and even the children were set gleaning the last handfuls of corn.

When the first alterations had been completed, Targett began to think he would do well to buy himself a small stock of poultry and even a pig, and so lighten his butcher's bill. There were peelings and household scraps enough to go most of the way towards keeping a pig, while the grass in front of the inn, and the stream beside it, offered pasturage and recreation for three or four geese. Targett had no sooner decided on this addition than he asked who had goslings to sell in those parts, and hearing that Mr. Sturmey was the man, he took his hat and stick, and went over to his farmhouse which, surrounded by a little hamlet called Newbarrow Boys, was at a distance of some two miles, and halfway to the next village Tarrant.

This was indeed almost the first time Targett had gone abroad from his public house, so busy had he been with his repairs.

As he walked he looked about him with pleasure. First came the village, then on higher ground the church, and when that was passed the road took a sharp turn and all was out of sight except the high downs on either side of him, now golden with fields of ripe waving corn, or white with stubble, up to the top of the chalk, or very near it. In many of the fields the harvesters were working, and he wondered how they could build their waggon-load of sheaves to stand up on the sides of hills so perilously steep. Indeed there were places there where the harvest was got in with extreme difficulty, and where the sheaves had to be carried by hand to the waggons, across the whole breadth of the field.

Presently he was come to the farmhouse, where he looked about him but saw no one stirring. There was not even a yard dog left to salute him; the folk were away on the down harvesting, and the door of the farmhouse was opened to his knock by a tall woman dressed in the handsomest style, a silk gown, a lace cap and a lace-trimmed apron—the farmer's wife for certain, though her attire was more suited to the grand lady of a manor house.

No sooner had Targett set eyes on her than a kind of wonder came into his face and he stood for a moment looking at her silently. And she also stood looking at him with amazement.

"Surely you are Lucy and my own sister," said Targett at length.

"And you William, come back from sea."

"I was seeking to buy some goslings, and now I have found you so near a neighbour. You are married then sister, I take it, to this farmer here."

"Yes, I am Mrs. Sturmey."

"Well Lucy, kiss me. It is long since our last meeting and the quarrel we had on that day seems unimportant now."

"That is true William, but first I must ask you a question: It is you who are the innkeeper at Maiden Newbarrow? And is it true that you have brought home a black woman and her child?"

"Aye. I brought my Tulip with me sister; what would you have me do? Indeed I left the sea because of my Tulip."

"How can you keep her here William? The scandal has already been talked about, and everywhere people say it is most shameful. They blame Mr. Stingo for letting the house to such a tenant. You must send her back, William; if she does not stay long I daresay it will be forgotten. Until then I cannot pretend to welcome you as our neighbour, though I bear you no ill-feeling for the past."

Targett recoiled a step while his sister was speaking, and gazed at her with a peculiar expression. Then he shook his head and said: "You have not changed much Lucy. You are the same as ever, but you should know me well enough to know that you cannot wheedle me."

Then he laughed. "Send away Tulip, Lucy, because you are such a fine lady! Why, my Tulip was a grander lady than you have ever seen, in Africa, and she brought me a great fortune. Why the inn itself is Tulip's and all that's in it; and as for you Lucy, you can tell your husband to send elsewhere for his beer. He shall have none from me unless to please me he turn you away. For I cannot abide the disgrace of such a heartless woman being my sister."

When he had said this he walked away from the farm, and began singing a chanty with bawdy words in it, and so got home without his geese, but with only a piece of knowledge which he would rather not have had. Indeed meeting with that fine lady, his sister, seemed to him an evil omen, and from that moment on Targett was ready to perceive any bad signs for the future which might have escaped his eyes before.

Nor were these altogether lacking, though many of them were so slight that the sailor would say all was imagination on his part and nothing more. Then he would utter an oath, pour himself out a glass of sherry, toss it off and go about his work with a pleasant smile, all happiness again.

The things which would so move him were trivial enough—a couple of women standing in the road to watch Tulip with evil in their faces, an urchin calling out: "Black sheep, black sheep, have you any wool?" or a stray word spoken by the men when he was out of the bar, yet overheard.

But these things were soon dismissed from his mind, and even when he most strongly resented them, he always managed to argue himself out of his ill temper.

"After all," he said to himself, "my Tulip is a black and woolly-headed negro, such as none of these bumpkins here could look at without wonder. 'Tis natural they should find her strange, and should stare at her open-mouthed. No one likes what is out of the ordinary. Everyone's first thought is to do it a mischief, and I must not blame them for that. But when they get used to seeing her all will be well; until then I must be careful, and she shall not walk through the village except when I am there with her."

Then it came into his mind that very soon he must do what he had been putting off day after day, ever since he had been in England, and that was visit London. His business there was to obtain a sum of money in cash by the sale of pearls and a little gold dust. This he had hoped to do without going to London, but he saw it was business outside the province of any country town. So thinking it over, Targett said to himself: "Aye, to London I must go, a city which I have never been in although I am an Englishman who has travelled over the whole world. And London is a port too; yet I have never chanced to sail from it."

Afterwards he spoke to Tulip, telling her why he must go to London and what a great city it was, and bid her live in the inn in a very retired way until his return.

Tulip listened to all he said very submissively, only saying to him at the end: "William, you do wrong to be jealous of me. You misjudge me if you think there is anyone among your white men here whom I should like to meet; no, I despise them all as much as I did all the black men in Africa. I love no one in the world but you William."

This mistaking of his meaning touched Targett's heart, for he had been thinking of her safety and had cautioned her not to expose herself lest anyone should do her an ill turn, either by throwing a stone, or by insulting her. Of all men Targett was least inclined to be jealous, and as is so often the case with men who are not jealous by nature, there was never any occasion for him to be so.

For jealousy is the cause of half the infidelity in the world, and if once a man find it has gained an entrance to his heart, he should clap his hand instantly to his forehead and cry out: "What have I here?" It is ten to one he will find a budding pair of horns.

"Well Tulip," answered Targett; "think me jealous if you will, but stay these three days indoors, lest some mischief be done you. For I have an enemy not far off who might insult you, and the louts here might pelt you with stones or filth."

And then he told her about his sister, and how even as boy and girl they had hated each other, of their last quarrel before he went to sea, and of their meeting again with one another at the door of her husband's farmhouse.

Tulip listened to what he said, and then shook her head and slapped it as if she hoped to beat some understanding into it—but still she could only wag her head, frown and look puzzled. At last she said:

"I cannot understand about your sister. It is too hard for me."

Then she looked up and saw William was smiling at her, and so burst into a peal of happy laughter and hugged him, saying: "Your sister has not hurt you, I see that by your smiling, so let's puzzle no more about the naughty witch."

And letting go of William, Tulip danced about him, then suddenly stopped and asked him again about his journey, could he not take her with him, and a thousand other questions. Would he see the Queen there? Would he go and stay with her pretty husband Prince Albert? And she told William how the Queen had sent a large picture of herself and of the Prince Consort as a present to her father, and how she had always loved to look at it.

Before Targett set out on his journey he called Tom Madgwick aside and told him that he trusted him, and that he left Tulip and little Sambo in his care, and that if any harm came to them he would hold him responsible with his life. Then he cautioned Tom against giving it out that his master was gone to London. No, he should not think him further away than Poole, and should expect him back at any moment. Also he should not serve any man too freely in the bar with spirits, but should put him off by saying there was none left in the bottle, and his master had taken the key of the cellar with him.

Poor Tom Madgwick was greatly troubled by William's foresight against what seemed to him impossible calamities, and for sometime after he had been given these confidential instructions he vexed his spirit by thinking them over. For the potman had an open ingenuous nature; he would never think ill of anyone, nor even suspect a strange dog of wishing to bite him, if it came up to him, and the hair bristling all down its back. Yet he did not think his master had been joking when he had warned him to be so much on his guard. No, he was certain that it was no jest when Targett told him that he would hold him responsible for Tulip's safety with his life. At last by thinking about the matter Tom hit upon a good explanation and then he went to Tulip and said to her: "Mrs. Tulip, I think Mr. Targett was a long time out of England."

"Yes Tom, I have heard him say so."

"He has been a good while among savages and black people hasn't he?"

"Why yes Tom, he has lived among us in Africa."

"He has often been in danger, perhaps even in danger of his life, hasn't he?"

"No Tom, what you would think great dangers are nothing to him. There is nothing in the world that is strong enough to hurt him. The sea cannot drown him; the fire cannot burn him; the lion cannot wound him with his paw; nor the elephant trample him with his feet. When he walks through the forest the snakes hide in holes and the panthers look the other way."

"Yes, I should think that he gave as good as he got," said Tom.

"I tell you," said Tulip with her eyes sparkling, "I have seen him ride upon a crocodile as if it were a horse; he put a chain in its mouth as a bridle, and so guided it and kept it from the river."

"I'll be blowed," said Tom, "then he isn't a man to be frightened of his own shadow, and yet there are no crocodiles here in Dorset, and he may have forgotten that in England we lead quiet lives and hardly have a riot in ten years."

After that Tom kept a sharp look-out for any mischief that might be intended, and spent half an hour in locking up and barring the house every night.

Nobody tried to break in, and his trouble was thrown away. Targett was absent four days, and when he returned half an hour after sunset the house seemed to him to be looking wonderfully sweet and peaceful, the very house he had wished for all along, so he jumped off the new horse, which he had bought in Dorchester, and would have called out to Tom to come and take it, but at that moment he heard the sound of someone playing his concertina. Now Tulip had never learnt to play the instrument, the reason being that she had a little pipe or rustic flute of her own, on which she would pick out her own savage tunes, and even make shift to accompany Targett when he sang sometimes, for she was musical.

"Can that be Tulip?" Targett asked himself, and then, throwing the bridle over a post of the fence, he walked to the end window, for the sound came from the parlour.

There through the window he saw a stranger, all alone in the room, with the concertina in his hands.

While Targett watched him the door opened and in came Tulip, who seeing her master's face against the window ran forward and threw it open. Meanwhile the man put down the concertina and Tulip said:

"Here is your brother come to see you William."

It was Targett's younger brother Harry, who had not seen him since he was fifteen years old. William greeted him, and Harry cried out:

"Well William, I am glad to see you; you have a fine place here and I am glad you have come back from sea. Tulip has entertained me well, and I must congratulate you on that young rogue Sambo."

Harry Targett was a young man with a high ringing voice, and fair hair which grew so thick that no barber could keep it to a parting. His complexion was pale; his eyes shining; there was a marked Adam's apple in his throat.

"Where have you sprung from Harry?"

"Only think," cried Tulip, "he rode up to the house to have a pint of ale; I looked out thinking it might be you, and then I heard him ask

Tom at the bar: 'Are you Mr. Targett?' And then; 'Is he a seafaring man about thirty?'"

"Tom was shy of answering me at first," said Harry, "but when I said you were my brother he softened, and Tulip came running in and made me wait here for the night in the hope that you would come back."

Targett threw off his coat, and Tulip had to exclaim again and again at the new clothes he had bought in London. Then while he drew off his riding boots she spied a gold watch-chain and seals hanging out from his fob. Targett drew it out and tossed it to her, a gold hunter watch, set with diamonds. He pulled off his gloves, and there was a fine belcher ring on his finger.

"I have some pretty trifles for you too, Tulip," he said, and pulled out a cheap necklace and a bracelet of gold.

"And there are lots of fine things coming from town, for I have done the greatest stroke of business you have ever heard of, and I'm a rich man Harry."

"I will say," he added patting Tulip on the head, "that I owe all my riches to Tulip here."

Tom came in then to call them to dinner, which was of a big crab apiece, followed by ducklings with green peas. They drank claret, which Tom was sent to fetch up from the cellar.

All through dinner Targett kept asking a thousand questions of his brother Harry. How were John and Mrs. John and what new nephews and nieces had he got? And how was Dolly? She must be a fine girl now—and what of the baby Francis? How was he? And how many of the old pastures had they broken up for corn? All these questions and the answers to them are not to the purpose of the story, only they filled up dinner. Then when they went back to the parlour with some old brandy, and while Tulip was fetching their pipes, Harry turned the tables.

"Nothing much happens on a farm William," said he; "that was the reason you gave our brother John for going to sea, and that is why I often think myself of going away to America. There is gold in California, and there are vast plains covered with wild horses and buffaloes and Indians. But what have you been doing these last ten years, William? For I am sure it is ten years since you came back to visit us. It is your turn now, and you must tell me your story."

"Drink up your brandy," said the sailor. "Go Tom," he shouted through the doorway; "go and burn us a pint of brandy. I shall have to wet my throat if I am to spin you such a long yarn.

"It was in forty-eight that I left home for the third time. I shipped at Bristol in the *Belsize,* barque, as second mate. We were carrying a cargo of Birmingham goods for Guinea, to return laden with log-wood and cocoa.

"I stayed in the *Belsize* for she suited me, and the Guinea trade was a change from southern seas and long cruises. In fifty-one, when I had been three years in the *Belsize* and was mate, we touched at Whydah, and I was sent ashore with a boat's crew to see if the merchants there could help us to make up a cargo. We had been disappointed at Lagos; Whydah was out of our usual beat. My men soon got into mischief in the town, and to stop further trouble in a strange port I marched them back to the coast and sent them on board, telling them to fetch me the next day, as the chacha, Mr. de Souza, had offered me hospitality.

"In the night a regular hurricane blew up and the *Belsize* had to slip her ground tackle and be off without me. That did not worry me, for I expected her to come back in the next few days and pick me up, when the sea had gone down a bit. However the weather continued wild for over a fortnight, and Captain Johnson, having been driven getting on for a thousand miles of his way home, thought it better to do without me then, meaning I suppose to come back for me on his next voyage, some two or three months later.

"He never came, for the *Belsize* was cast away on Lundy Island in a fog. I wrote of course to the owners by the next vessel out from Whydah, and they treated me very handsomely, for they wrote back sending me my wages and compensation money. Living at Whydah I was two miles from the sea and out of sight they say means out of mind.

"Whydah you know is the chief town still left in the slave trade, though that of course is nothing now to what it was once. Being an Englishman, I was looked on with suspicion by all the merchants except one, a Mr. Martinez, who treated me very kindly, and in whose house I stayed when I had no money. It so happened that a Brazilian ship put in after I had been living in the town about six months, and the Captain was taken very ill with rheumatism. They were in want of an officer to take his place, as he was the only competent navigator on board of her. I had often asked Mr. Martinez how I could repay him for all his kindnesses. He had an interest in this Brazilian ship, which was nothing more nor less than a slaver, and now he came to me and said: 'Oh Captain Targett, why were you born an Englishman? I would to Heaven you were a man of any other country; however there is no help for it.' This was as good as asking me to run the boat over to Bahia for him, and seeing his distress, I offered myself. I did that to oblige him, but knowing it is a dangerous sort of trade, and that it is criminal for an Englishman to employ himself in it, I would not continue after that one voyage, although the handsomest offers were made to me to do so; neither would I take any money from Mr. Martinez for that trip. The Brazilian captain having recovered when I got back loaded with rum, I was the better able to decline all the propositions made to me. After that voyage I was once more at Whydah, but of course on a very different footing. On several occasions I went to the capital, Abomey, in the company of Mr. Martinez and by him was presented to His Sable Majesty King Gaze-oh. You know Harry, I was afraid to be at Whydah after that voyage to the Brazils. Her Majesty's ship *Kingfisher* was often enough in the roads, and her captain had heard of what I had done, he might demand me from the viceroy, or even kidnap me away. I had no mind to be transported to Botany Bay as a slaver and a renegade. For that reason I decided to move to Abomey. While I was there I fell a good deal into the company of old King Gaze-oh. He was every inch a king and a very good friend to me, and it was he who gave me his daughter Gundemey, whom I call Tulip, in marriage, who otherwise would have been a captain in his army of Ama-johns, as they call them on the coast. After I had been living there two years, Gaze-oh was taken ill with the small-pox and died, leaving the kingdom to his son Geleley. When a king dies in that part of the world there is a very great slaughter made of the women in the palace so that he shall not go alone. On his death-bed Gaze-oh made everyone swear to forgo this massacre; but yet I felt no security because Geleley and I were not suited to one another, and he was the king. At such times it is hard to tell what that people will not do, so the day before Gaze-oh died I left Abomey and went back to Whydah, to Mr. Martinez, and through him got safe passage to Portugal with Tulip and Sambo. Everyone on the coast knew I had married old Gaze-oh's daughter, so I dressed Tulip in man's clothes and kept Sambo hidden while I was on an English ship. They were not likely to be on the look out for me, but I took no chances. Tulip had brought me eighty slaves as her dowry so that I was a rich man whilst at Abomey, though dependent on the favour of the king. But leaving so suddenly I could only carry with me that part of Tulip's fortune which was in pearls and gold-dust and ivory, yet that has fetched more than five hundred pounds, enough to get me a hulk of my own."

"You'll not be off to sea again, surely," said Harry.

"No. I've got my Tulip and little Sambo and this public house here, what I call my hulk, and now I shall live here happily to the end of my days."

"What sort of a place is that town you spoke of?" asked Harry.

"Abomey lies less than a hundred miles from the sea, in country which has a wondrous soft and pleasant aspect, all fields of corn dotted with palm orchards. The chief fault in its situation is that there is very little drinking water, and that is oftentimes white with clay. In the town there are many great palaces; I lodged in one of them. They are all thatched houses like here in Dorset, with clay walls, but the thatch comes within a few feet of the ground. The Komasi palace has two stories, the others only one. Everything in Abomey is given up to the king and his army. But you will never believe me now Harry, when I tell you that the army is half women, and they are more feared than are the men. There are five or six thousand of these women in Dahomey, and if Gaze-oh had not let me marry her Tulip would have been one of them, for she was in the band of archers, who are young girls. The older women are all armed with muskets like our own foot soldiers in the Crimea.

"Once a year, in January, the king holds his own customs, and then after that the bush-king holds his. By some Gaze-oh and the bush-king are thought to be the same man. That is what I say, but Tulip always says no. At the king's customs all evil-doers are slain and the palace steps are planted with human heads. That is a terrible time and the town runs red with blood. Yet even then everything in the kingdom is only a kind of play-acting, for they are an exceedingly happy people; drinking, dancing, singing, those are the ways they pass the time; all is no more than dressing themselves up, one day as leopards, the next as bulls; and yet in the middle of their fun they will be cruel and blood-thirsty. Tulip was so much a favourite that I was privileged for her sake, and saw only the lighter side of life. They are the merriest people and care for nothing so much as dancing, and rum, and women, and masquerades. The women are more the equals of the men than here in England. You cannot imagine that Harry. While I was there I drank enough for six, though sometimes I would go forth with a party to hunt elephants for the ivory or to capture slaves.

"It was my first hunt of that kind that brought me Tulip. The king went out with a large party into the bush taking me with him, but he was seized with a colic, and lay in his tent with no taste for hunting. He sent for me then and told me I should not miss seeing the sport, because he was a little indisposed, and that seven of his Ama-johns were setting out, and that I should go with them in charge of an eunuch. These huntresses were the elder women, great fat things, but as strong as oxen, and all of them noted shots. Each one carried an elephant gun, and had a young girl with her to carry her bag of bullets and to wait on her. Tulip was one of these. We were crossing a belt of open country, covered with patches of tall, dry grass, and we went in a long line like beaters to rouse any game there might be. I was at the end of the line, and Tulip was next to me and beyond her the huntress she served. I was just in the thick of some tall grass when they roused an elephant at the other end of the line and fired at him. But instead of there being one brute, there was a herd. When I got out of the patch of long grass I was in, I saw twenty or thirty of the great beasts charging up and down the line and throwing headless bodies in the air, for the first thing your elephant does is to pull off the head. I drew back into the tall grass at once, and lay there, while the brutes trampled up and down round the bodies of the women; they stayed there trumpeting till long after sunset.

"At last the sound of their feet and of their cries died away in the distance. The moon was full, and the brightness of it extraordinary even for the tropics. When I put my head out of the grass and looked about me the first thing I saw was Tulip, not twenty yards off, doing the same thing. When she saw me she came out, and took me by the hand, for she was glad to see anyone at that moment.

"I for my part was equally joyful, and took her in my arms and kissed her, without thinking that it was an act that would have cost me my life had there been anyone there to see. Tulip was thirteen years old then, a pretty creature, not quite formed as a woman, for she was more backward than most of her race.

"Together we searched for the others, but found no one, only dark patches in the trampled grass, a broken gun and the carcasses of three elephants. We dared not search long, for there were lions, leopards and hyænas all about us, drawn to the spot by the smell of blood, and the meat of the dead elephants. The roaring and screaming of these creatures was hideous, but we passed through them safely, and slept unmolested in the open country. The air was cold, and Tulip lay very close to me, with her arms about my chest for warmth; she had lost her mantle and was bare above the waist. The next evening we got back to King Gaze-oh's camp, and by that time Harry, I had conceived a very great affection for the child. We found that three of the other girls, and one Ama-john, were just got back. They were the only other survivors. I went directly to the king, where he lay on a couch in his tent. When he heard my story he showed very great concern, not for the loss of his huntresses, but for Tulip.

"'Captain William, Captain William,' he cried, (for that was the name I used after my cruise to the Brazils) 'what shall I do now? The poor girl is undone; how can I save her? I know they will all whisper that you ravished her. I know that they will demand her head when I keep my customs.' Then he began to curse Dahomey, and his ancestors and his people, saying that they were the most cruel, savage and bloodthirsty scoundrels in the world, and that there was no ruling them without perpetual slaughter. I had heard him say a great deal to the same purpose on a former occasion, so that his words did not surprise me as much as they would otherwise have done. At last I told him that if he would give me Tulip I would convey her secretly out of his kingdom and that I would marry her.

"'If you will take her,' said he, 'you will save the poor girl's life without flying the country either, but I would not wish you to have her Captain William for your own sake.' I asked him what he meant by that, and he answered that he could not give me his daughter except honourably, and then I should be his son, and as much accountable to him as any of his family, and that if I used Tulip ill I should have to answer for it with my head, and that being a white man would not save me from the most horrible of deaths. I told him that I would run those risks willingly, only to have his daughter even if there were no question of her life, for I loved the child, and had no doubt I should love the woman. All the while we were talking thus Tulip sat in one corner of the king's tent, cutting a thorn out of her foot, and never looking my way or saying a word to her father. At last he turned to her and asked if she would trust herself with a white man, and said many things in my commendation. Tulip still sat puzzling over the thorn in her foot. When her father had said all he could think of (and that was a great deal more than was necessary) she said: 'I must first get this broken thorn out of my foot father.'

"Old Gaze-oh laughed at that, and we waited her pleasure. At last she put away her knife very carefully, got on to her feet and looked me up and down for a few moments, and then she said: 'Yes, I will have him.' After that she took me by the hand and said: 'You are a very big man Captain William, to be my husband; otherwise I like you well enough as I think you must know already.'

"Well, well, it is a great change Harry, to be here. Tulip feels it to be sure ten times more than I do; for her everything is as strange as it was for me in her father's kingdom. But our folk are not so merry as the Africans are, and that makes the greatest change for her, as she is used to laughter. Often she has asked me why the men here do not dance, why they never beat drums, or clap their hands, or shout songs in chorus. She thinks we are a very dull set of dogs here."

While William was speaking Tulip knelt in the corner, sitting back on her heels. It was strange to see her there in her English dress, with a full skirt, and her head bare, with its crop of short and curly wool.

"Do you remember William, at the bush-king's customs, how they sang?"

And then Tulip began to sing a gay song of her own country.

"Take off those clothes child," said William, "and dance for us." Tulip rose obediently and left the room. When she came back she was dressed strangely enough in what she thought came nearest to the costume of her own country; this was indeed nothing but a pair of white calico drawers held in place by a gaily-coloured silk scarf which William had given her. Round her head she had wound a band of broad white tape as a fillet. Her figure was very slender, her body very black. She was tattoed under the breasts on her belly. "Nay Tulip," said William, "I fear you will scandalize Harry. He is not used as I am to seeing you black women without your clothes."

Tulip was offended by these words, her lip trembled, her eyes filled with tears. For she was naturally modest, and such a reflection upon her behaviour wounded her. She caught up her little jacket and slipped it on at once, but William had no sooner spoken than he was sorry for his words. Harry however had taken them as a capital joke and laughed out aloud. In laughing he choked, spilt some brandy and laughed again. "Silly girl, I was only joking with you," said William. "The less you wear the better you look."

Tulip could never resist laughter; she was never sulky long, so that very soon she had forgiven William for what had angered her. Then she threw off her jacket, blew Harry a kiss, and called to William for music. What followed cannot be described, for a dance has to be seen with the eye; no words can imitate the dancer's gestures. Here it must suffice to say that William played his concertina, while at the same time he marked the tune by beating with his heel on a tin teatray, and that this teatray, put upside down on the floor, served very well for a drum. Whilst he did this he also sang, if one can call it singing, the chorus of a negro song, which, sometimes high and sometimes low, came in again and again. Tulip began her entertainment by throwing a few cartwheels, and by pulling a great many extravagant faces, which sent Harry into fits of laughter. After this opening she began the regular Dahomian dance to William's accompaniment. In this the whole body is incessantly agitated, the hands saw the air, the elbows are jerked back and forth so violently as to click together behind the back like the slow measure of castanets, the breasts tremble and shake, whilst the feet stamp, kick, and shuffle, and the hips and buttocks move to and fro, round and round, backwards and forwards, all marking perfect time to the music, thus forming the most harmonious and edifying spectacle it is possible to imagine, that is if the performer is young and pretty. Every now and then as she danced Tulip called out: "Faster, William, faster!" and the dance became more violent and more rapid. At last William gave a cry of exhaustion, and threw himself back panting in his chair. Tulip brought the dance to an end by walking across the room on her hands, while William marked every step with a loud bang on the teatray. Tulip's body was glistening with sweat like a horse after a sharp gallop, but she was not winded as William was, and after throwing a shawl over her shoulders she began to sing herself.

So with Tulip sometimes singing and sometimes dancing while William played the concertina, they passed the hours of the night. Every little while Harry and William would take another glass of brandy grog. Now and then Tulip would take a sip, not too much, lest it should make her giddy.

Tulip's childhood had been passed, as William had told his brother, in a royal palace, and she had been taught the proper deportment for a king's daughter. No gracious feat of the body or trick of dancing had been omitted from her education.

After sometime William wished to dance himself; he gave Harry the concertina, while he showed them a good hornpipe. After that he danced as Tulip had done, but he was not so perfect as she.

Harry stopped playing, his last glass of brandy had been too much for him, and when he stood up to stretch himself he staggered and would have fallen had not William caught him by the shoulder.

They led him to his bed; he tumbled into it and fell fast asleep.

But though William had come that day from London, and had ridden out from Dorchester to Maiden Newbarrow, and although he had been drinking quite as heavily as his brother, Harry, his head was moderately clear, and his appetite for pleasure was unquenched.

"Come along Tulip," he cried. "See, it is a clear night; we will ride over the hill to the sea."

They went down then to the stable, fetched out William's new riding horse, and the one on which Harry had been mounted, saddled them and rode off.

The sky was already pale, and the horses, excited at being taken out at an hour strange to them, galloped down the road and straight through the village street.

William halloed as they passed the church, and Tulip answered with a loud cry, which you may be certain had never been heard before in Dorset.

When they had already passed some way into the open country, there was a scratching of lucifers, a snapping of flint on steel, then a rushlight or two, and a candle gleamed in the windows of the village as the old women looked out into the pale street.

William and Tulip soon passed Lucy's farm, and breasted the down beyond.

Over the hill was the sea. There they went cautiously down a winding path that led them to the gap in the cliffs. Soon they dismounted, tied their horses to a tree and ran down onto the beach.

It was high tide, and the sea was so calm that it might have been a great saucer of milk; gently moving but without a wave it brimmed up to the very lip of the shingle beach.

William threw off his coat, his shirt and his trousers.

"Are there no sharks?" asked Tulip.

"No, not in England."

Tulip had slipped on her seaman's trousers, and an old coat of William's when she came riding. Now she flung them off and raced after him into the water. It was warmer to their bodies than the air of the August night.

They swam out in silence, Tulip's curly black head bobbing in the wake of William's fair one.

The coolness of the sea and the salt taste to it sobered William, and the excitement of his journey, of meeting with Harry, and the singing, the dancing, the music and the ride, vanished. The fumes of brandy departed suddenly; he felt calm and at peace.

They swam back. As they got into their clothes William said:

"Glad we got away from Dahomey, Tulip?"

"I too am glad," answered Tulip.

"Your father was a good man all the same," said William as they untied the horses.

"Yes," said Tulip as they went up the cliff road. "His ghost cannot follow us here. Don't let's speak of him."

When they got back to Maiden Newbarrow the men had gone to work, the women were getting ready breakfast against their return; they stared at Tulip, who rode in front with her bare feet thrust into the leathers of Harry's stirrups, William's jacket hanging loosely in folds round her naked body, and her wet, woolly head shining.

Targett gave them each a cheerful "Good morning," but they did not answer until he turned towards them in his saddle.

Tom came running out and took their horses. Harry was still asleep and did not get up till past midday.

Then he embraced Tulip, wrung William's hand and mounted his horse.

"I must get on to our sister Lucy's," said he; but in less than an hour he was back again.

"It seems I must choose between Lucy and Tulip, William. That's the greeting I got at the farm. She had heard of our jollification last night. So I told her straight out that I thought it was better to be black outside like Tulip than foul within like herself."

William laughed and asked Harry to come in, but Harry would not stay, he only bared his teeth in a grin which matched Tulip's own, waved his hand, set spurs to his horse, and was off to the home farm on the other side of the county.

Harry's words gave William a great deal of pleasure; he went about his business the next few days in high spirits, and began making a weathercock in the form of a full-rigged ship with all her canvas set.

But if he had not been so happy and high-spirited, whistling and singing as he cut out the sails, masts, and rigging, in the sheet of copper, and afterwards polishing it, smoothing it, painting the sails white, the hull vermilion, and gilding the little figurehead, he must have observed a new surliness in the villagers. The men still came for their beer, as was natural, but the women did not speak to him when he went through the village.

By this time little Sambo was quite firm on his legs, and was always running in and out of the house. His mother was very gentle with him, and never scolded him in the harsh and strident way that the village women use to their children. But in a low voice she would reason with him when he was at fault, or so laughingly chide him that he was easily disposed to alter his ways for the better.

As a result of her tender treatment there was never a child of Sambo's years that cried so little, or that had shed so few tears during its young life. He was indeed the most merry fellow imaginable, smiling at everyone he saw, though he had a certain shyness too, which made him keep his distance from strangers. Often he would stand in the doorway of the bar and smile winningly at any of the men who spoke to him, yet he would not trust himself to go to them when they called him, but only laugh and wag his head and hesitate.

Tulip made it her practice to go out with her child part of every morning. Then she would let him run where he would, and idly wander after the child, and often stand still for ten minutes at a stretch watching him play, and hold out her hand for her baby to come and take it. Sometimes they would wander into the village, but usually they went out on the other side from it, and then perhaps they would turn into a green meadow where she could sit down.

All the while Tulip was watching lest Sambo should run into some danger, and she kept her eyes open, though chiefly for dangers which are not to be met with in Dorset. Thus her glance always scanned the sky for eagles and vultures, the hedges for leopards and wild cats, and the ground itself for venomous serpents and noxious deadly insects. The only dangerous creatures which she and Sambo were ever likely to meet were the bulls, which in Dorset-shire are not shut up but go usually with the cows, and the rare vipers which were not often to be found so near to the village.

Sambo might it is true, get stung by a nettle or a wasp, but there were no scorpions or poisonous spiders; he might prick his fingers on the spines of a straying hedgehog, but there were no angry porcupines to slap him full of quills with a smack of their tails. And as for lions, leopards, bears, baboons, and crocodiles, there was nothing of that kind. Tulip might surely have closed her eyes; her child was safe enough in England.

Yet even so the negress found something to disquiet her, for one day she brought back Sambo early, walking faster than was usual with her, and looking round to see if she were followed. Targett was outside the inn, varnishing his new weathercock before setting it up, and he noticed her unusual step and her agitation, and hailed her:

"Tulip my girl, what is wrong this morning? Why do you look so?"

At first Tulip would not speak at all, but knowing her well Targett showed no impatience, only he set down his masterpiece, the full-rigged ship, and went to her and took her by the shoulder and kissed her poor black face, and ran his fingers through her woolly hair.

So wheedling her, at length he got her to tell him her story; but even then she would only whisper it fearfully to him, as if afraid that someone would overhear her, though there was no one even in sight, and they stood together in an open space where no eavesdropper could come nigh them.

"William," said she, "I am very afraid for Sambo. The Black Doctor came up to me in the road just now, and I am afraid of him. He will do Sambo a mischief."

Targett was used to her speech, which came from her African ways of thinking, and so when she said "the Black Doctor," he understood her to mean nothing worse than the village parson, the Rev. Adrian Cronk.

"Why do you fancy that Tulip?" he asked her. "What did the parson do to you that you should be afraid of him on Sambo's account?"

"He came up to me as I was standing in the road," answered Tulip whispering. "And he asked me what was the name of my little boy. I told him: 'Mr. Targett calls him Sambo.'"

"Then he said you could not give him a name unless he was washed in the church, and after that was done he would be as white as snow. And unless we had him washed white Sambo would be burnt in a fire with devils."

And then poor ignorant Tulip gave way completely and burst into loud sobs. For a long while nothing Targett could say or do would comfort her, and she only broke out afresh into pitiful moans and blubbering whenever he spoke. When he tried to take her into his arms she would have pushed him away, but that he held her fast.

And little Sambo, seeing his mother so distracted, ran up to her and hid himself in her skirts, and began to wail and whimper himself to keep her company.

William then led her indoors and forced her to drink a can of beer, and argued with her soberly, and at last dried her tears.

But when he told her that what the parson said was true, and that children in England were always christened, her tears gushed forth again and she became quite distracted.

At last Targett got out of her what was at the bottom of her troubles, for she blubbered out:

"I want to keep my Sambo. I am black and I love my black baby. I shall never love him the same after he is washed white."

Targett then could scarcely forbear laughing at her for her heathen notion, and told her that Sambo would always be the same colour; the parson could not change that whatever he did. But for a long time Tulip would not believe him, and at last she said:

"If I am washed, can I be made white also? I would not mind so much then, but perhaps William you would not love me if I were not black."

At this Targett had to laugh outright. But although he laughed, he kissed her, and presently persuaded her that she had misunderstood the whole matter, though she still continued fearful of the effects of a baptism and convinced that the Black Doctor might be a danger to Sambo.

It was beyond the sailor's power to explain to Tulip the true nature of redemption. For not only was he by his habit of life naturally indifferent to religion, but he was somewhat hazy upon such matters as original sin, and even the communion itself. All he knew or could tell Tulip was that he was a Christian, that what was good enough for him should be good enough for her and for his children, and now they were in England and not in Africa, and must live according to the English religion.

He told her, too, that here in Dorset there was only one God; and that he had written a book in which he had set down the early history of the world, which was called "The Holy Bible." There was a second part of it, called "The New Testament" which contained the life of Jesus Christ, Who was the Son of God by a virgin, and that all our sins had been taken over by Christ, provided always that we believed in Him.

But while William told Tulip these things, it was apparent to her that he did not lay very much store by them, and was not a bit afraid of the fire of which the Black Doctor had spoken. Indeed William told her that it was time enough to go to church and worry oneself about such matters when one was old and past work, but one must always show a proper respect for the parson.

All this allayed Tulip's first terrors very much, and gave rise to a singular notion in her head, and that was that the English God was nothing like so powerful or dangerous as the African gods to whom she was accustomed. For even her father, who was a king, trembled at the name of the Porro-men. No one in Dahomey could have said like her William that there was no need to worry about religion until one was old.

There the gods or devils (call them whichever you please) were so strong that their worshippers could have anything they desired, and in particular the Snake God and the Leopard God were powerful above the others. Almost everyday a man was suddenly changed by one or other of these gods into a leopard or a snake, and would snatch up a child and carry him off in his jaws while the mother and father were powerless to resist.

And in the evening the man who had been changed into the form of a beast would be back at his house in his own shape, and all his fellow worshippers would be invited to partake of the sacred roast.

It was natural therefore, that Tulip should have many questions to ask concerning the Holy Sacrament, and Transubstantiation, but she soon found that it was nothing like what she had imagined it to be. This you may be sure was a very great consolation to her, yet the sight of the parson Mr. Cronk, and the tolling of the church bells on a Sunday, always made poor heathen Tulip uneasy and secretly afraid that someone or other of the churchwardens in the form of a beast would pounce upon her or upon her Sambo.

This conversation was not to be left without fruit, though William dismissed it for the time being from his mind, for about a week or two later Mr. Molten, one of the farmers, was in the bar, and asked him point blank had he had the child baptized yet?

"No," said William, "there's plenty of time for that."

"You have no call to name the child Sambo then," said the farmer. "I can call him young Sea-Coal or what I like and it's as much his name as Sambo is."

"But he answers to me when I call him Sambo," said William, and just then Sambo ran in so pertly that he made them all burst out laughing.

"Well," said the farmer, "I think young Sea-Coal is the better name for him, but whether it is Sea-Coal or Sambo, you'll have to have him christened if you are to live here and bring him up with our children at the school. We can't have him teaching them to worship heathen idols."

William laughed at this, and said he would speak to the parson about the christening one of these days.

It was autumn, the harvest was all gathered in, the hedges were covered with the last blackberries, and William began to make provisions for the winter when his public-house would be the meeting-place every night for all the men of the village. Foreseeing this, he prepared to throw open another room, which led out of the public bar, so that they should not be too crowded. He had the whole of the room newly painted, and put in a hatchway to the bar, so that the men could be served without leaving the room. Then thinking of the long winter evenings which were in store for all of them, he determined that there should be games in that room, so the men might play and keep amused.

First he painted a bull's head very like life, upon the wall in one corner, and drove a big hook into the wall between its nostrils. Then he found an old brass ring, just the ring that farmers use to put in the nose of a bull when he is young to hold him, and he fastened this ring to a line about five feet long and tied the other end to a staple in the ceiling so the ring hung freely. By swinging it with nice judgment, a man might get the ring to catch the hook, and so ring the bull. This game was one which Targett had heard say was the oldest parlour game in England, and it pleased him to have a sport of such antiquity in his bar. For the rest he had to go into Dorchester to buy a set of hooks and rings and parlour quoits, a target with darts, and a bagatelle table with two or three spare cues and balls, and a couple of sets of boxing gloves, for he thought every man ought to be able to use his fists. Besides these he planned to get a ruled slate with metal discs for shove-halfpenny, a box or two of dominoes, a draughts-board with men, and a bag of marbles with a board for fox and geese or solitaire. Armed with all these he thought he could make the winter pass pleasantly enough for his patrons, the village yokels and the farmers and their sons. Then there was another toy which he added himself and which caused as much amusement as any of the others, particularly when there were any strangers in the company. This was nothing more than a quantity of pith balls, which he made by forcing the pith out of the young branches of an elder bush, and then dried them and rounded them carefully with his razor. Many a pint of beer was won and lost with these pith balls, for although they looked large and solid to the eye, and seemed as though a man might throw them like pebbles, they were such featherweight things that they could not be thrown at all. The strongest man might take one in his hand and hurl it with all his might, but when the pith ball left his hand it fell gently to the ground not a yard away. But there was a trick with these, and that was to set open the doors on each side of the room and let the draught catch them, and then they would blow right across the room and out into the passage.

In this way William prepared to amuse and entertain the men who came to drink a quart of ale at his house. For he loved all pastimes and sports himself, and on board ship had always found that they sweetened the voyage and prevented arguments and quarrels, and the hatching of any kind of mischief, most of which comes about, so he would say, from dullness and lack of something to do. Everything Targett did he did himself, so instead of ordering these things to come out by the carrier he rode one day into Dorchester to choose them himself, so they should be of the best quality made and just as he fancied.

I cannot say how it was but one or two women seeing him ride away, dressed very sprucely in his best with a new top hat on his head, inquired of each other:

"Where was Mr. Targett going?"

Someone then gave it out that he was away to London, and this piece of news as they thought it, was spread by the means of an old woman selling buttons and combs, and got carried to Newbarrow Boys, where his sister Lucy lived in the farmhouse. From thence it got carried to the village beyond as a certain thing that Mr. Targett had gone away to London that morning.

When Targett got back to the village that night it was growing dark. Night falls before we expect it in the autumn; the traces of summer linger on into winter, and we resent the shorter hours of daylight all the more because there are still roses in the garden. But though it was dark it was not yet night; there was still a little colour in the sky held there by the storminess of the clouds, which though they lay torn in savage ribbons remained frozen, and immobile, yet threatening. It was impossible to judge their distance; they might have been near or very far away. William let his horse drop into a walk. A sky like that always told him stories, calling up memories of other skies, and of all the scenes which those other skies had brought with them. The sky which he had in his mind's eye was just such a one as he had been watching for the last half-hour, but it was a Patagonian one. It had foretold his first passage round Cape Horn. How angry the sea had been, how cold! His heart had failed him as he had walked the deck, but it had proved only a threat; the tempest had not broken, and a fortnight later he had picked an orange in a garden in Valparaiso while a pretty girl lay in a hammock and laughed at him.

There was the shrill sound of women shouting. William looked down from the sky, and for the first few moments his eyes could distinguish nothing in the darkness which hung over the earth. Figures were moving in front of the inn. There were two or three flashes like a flint struck on steel, then a flame which died away quickly. William pulled up his horse and listened. At intervals a woman screamed out a few words.

"Smoke them out." "Fire the thatch." "Bring out the black sheep." Then she shrieked more rapidly: "Oh, the dirty nigger! Come and give her a singeing boys! I'll make her dance, the ugly toad!" A man's voice said: "Best hand her out Tom, or they will fire the house; there is no holding them; they will have her."

William did not wait longer, but pressing his horse with his knees rode up at a gentle trot. As he approached he could see that there was a crowd gathered. Three or four figures were standing close in front of the inn, and all round at a little distance groups of silent figures were looking on. Targett rode straight up to the door of "The Sailor's Return." There was a silence.

"What's this neighbours?" he asked with his hunting crop in his hand. It was sometime before he got an answer, but at last one of the men on the outskirts of the crowd called out: "They have all come over from Newbarrow Boys; maybe your sister sent them."

"Yes, they all came from Newbarrow Boys and Tarrant about an hour ago," cried another man: "we were just watching them to see they didn't do any mischief."

"That Tom Madgwick is a bold fellow; when they went in the bar he drove them out with a gun in his hands and locked the door on them."

Targett found that the crowd seemed just as big as ever but it was composed of his friends.

"Tom—how is this?" said he, for by this time Tom had opened the door. "Is it true that they came from the next village?"

"Yes," said Tom; "I think the others only came to look on. They took no part either way."

"Well tell my sister Mrs. Sturmey, and her husband," said William, "that if ever this happens again, or if my Tulip should meet with any harm, that I hold them responsible, and shall spare no money to see them hanged." Then looking about him, he said: "Put away that gun Tom, what would you do if some of these good neighbours of ours died of fright? It would mean transportation for you. Goodnight my friends, no more of this nonsense or I shall make an example that we shall all be sorry for."

He found Tulip much calmer and more self possessed than any European woman would have been after such a riot. She was indeed contemptuous of them all, and said that she could not be afraid of that rabble. He found that she had filled all the buckets she could find at the well behind the house, while the villagers were threatening to set it afire at the front.

The next day all the games, the darts and target, hooks and rings, and the bagatelle board and so forth came out by the carrier and were delivered at the inn. But William, who had been choosing them with so much care the day before, and looking forward for several days to fitting up the new parlour with them, had no pleasure in them now. Indeed he would not even open the parcels, until Tulip, knowing what was inside, beseeched him to do so that she might play with them. If she had not said this it is most likely that William would not have set them up at all. For when he considered that all his care in making his inn a pleasant place was but to give pleasure to that crowd of people whom he had found outside it the day before, he was filled with a kind of disgust and anger and knew not what to do. In this perplexity of his he would not even serve the men who came in that morning himself, but left it to Tom, until suddenly he said aloud: "What, Billy? Daren't you show your nose on the bridge, because the crew mutiny? Or because the bumboat women last night were saucy to you? Are you only a fairweather commander?"

Saying that he went straight to the bar and told Tom to leave it to him. "I'll serve these gentlemen here myself." This he roared out in a voice that made the glasses ring and the men in the taproom start up with surprise. And in the same voice of thundering geniality he held forth on the weather, on the price people were getting for Michaelmas geese, and the new stores of liquor which he was laying in for the coming winter. This voice of his drowned any desire the men there might have had to speak about the events of the night before; it overawed them, and almost dazed them with admiration for a man who could call such tones out of his chest. None of the village people presumed either then or afterwards to speak to Targett about the scene of that night directly, but only alluded to it sideways, saying that "busybodies were a nuisance and old women who didn't mind their own affairs ought to be ducked in the stream." Or that: "there are plenty of stuck-up women who would pine and die away if they weren't always making mischief."

In a week or so the first blustering gale of autumn broke upon them, and kept them all indoors for three days, while outside the wind was howling and the rain streaming, and clouds hid the downs beyond the village. At the inn all was snug and warm, as well battened down as a ship in a gale. For those days they had a full house, and Tom had his work cut out to serve all the company. Targett made fires in both of the rooms, scattered sawdust, and sometimes opened a door to let a cloud of tobacco smoke out, and a puff of air come in. This was a great change for Tulip and gave her a foretaste of what it would be like in the winter. The house smelt of wet leather and corduroy, of heavy shag and of the beer drippings. Every now and then the door slammed, the house shook in a blast of wind, and then there would be a shout of greeting, a new buzz of talk and the jingle of coppers as Tom flung them into the drawer. All day long the bar was full of men drinking and talking; all day long she could hear the click of the bagatelle balls, or the tinkle of the ring striking against the hook on the bull's nose. The voices of the men subdued her; the smell from the bar sickened her.

During the day Tulip kept to the kitchen or the washhouse, and sat still with Sambo at her knee telling him stories. At night she felt better, her sickness left her, and as the quarter-hours struck on the grandfather clock her spirits rose. Soon the last maundering song would be ended, the last "Goodnight all" would ring out, the last stumbling drunkard would grope his way out of the passage, and the door would be locked and bolted. Then William would come into the kitchen, wiping the sweat off his neck, inside the collar of his shirt. He reeked with sweat and beer, and was moist all over with his work, his eyes were bloodshot with tobacco smoke; but happiness for Tulip began in the winter with closing time, after which she could gaze at William without restraint until he had staggered upstairs to their bedroom, had tumbled into bed and blown out the light.

After three days the rain was all spent, and though the wind continued for a while, the sun shone fitfully. The roads had been swept by water, leaving banks of clean sand and beds of polished gravel at the corners, while new channels at the side of the space in front of the inn revealed the force of the storm. The little stream was swollen to a brown and turbid river, which covered the stepping-stones. That morning, while Tom was having his dinner, and Targett was in the empty bar, there came a knock at the door which stood open and the parrot screamed out: "A pint of bitter, pint of bitter, sharp Tom, sharp." William went out in some surprise and found a visitor waiting on the doorstep, but a visitor who dared not enter the house. It was the parson, Mr. Cronk.

"Are you Targett, the new landlord here?" he asked.

"Come in," said William. "If you wish to speak to me, step inside."

"No, no," said the clergyman; "I was merely passing, just passing, and I wanted to drop you a hint Mr. Targett. I heard among my parishioners a rumour, it may be untrue, I hope you will be able to deny it—but a rumour that you had threatened Mrs. Sturmey."

William gazed at his visitor in astonishment.

The clergyman went on:

"You must withdraw that threat. I am responsible for the peace of the parish, and I cannot have you threatening my parishioners."

William looked at the clergyman and grinned. Then he nodded his head slowly and said:

"I did threaten them, Sir. I threatened everyone at Newbarrow Boys, and my sister Mrs. Sturmey and her husband in particular, with the law. If they assault my wife and child, burgle or set fire to my house, I shall have them hanged or transported by the officers of the law. I repeat that threat Mr. Cronk."

The clergyman looked up at William indignantly, but the sailor was grinning. A moment later Mr. Cronk recovered himself and said: "By the way Targett, I spoke to your, ahem, to your wife about the little negro boy."

"That is right," said William. "I was coming to see you about it, but I've been busy ever since I came here, with painting the house and one thing and another."

"Then you give your permission to have him christened and brought up as a Christian."

"I shall bring the child up to be a Christian like myself," said William, "and I shall send him to sea in a whaling vessel. He should make a good harpooneer."

"Goodday Targett," said the clergyman. William grinned again, turned and discovered Tulip, who had been eavesdropping, behind the door. There was in her face an expression of great alarm, mingled with relief, and coming on her suddenly like that, William burst out laughing, caught her by both hands and whirled her out onto the doorstep of the inn. As he did so, the parson turned and looked back, and Tulip catching sight of him gave a scream and ran into the house. This incident tickled William's sense of humour and he burst into peal after peal of laughter that rang noisily through the air and even startled the old women gossiping in the village street. William laughed and laughed again; he found he could not stop and leaned up against the door-post weakly. While he laughed, the Rev. Adrian Cronk looked about him in terror lest he should have been seen leaving the inn. People would think Targett was laughing at him. The parson did not dare walk into the village, and on the spur of the moment jumped down into the ditch and crawled behind the carrier's cartshed. There his coat was stuck all over with burdocks and cleavers, and his thumb scratched by a spray of bramble. His heart beat like a mill, everything whirled before his eyes, but he was happy for the moments he lay hidden; anything was preferable to walking through the village with that sailor laughing at him, and he was always happiest when only the eye of God was looking. He had never fancied God laughing at his creatures. When all was quiet, he peeped out, saw no one, and thinking himself secure, slipped out into the road.

The reverend gentleman had of course been observed taking cover, but it did not surprise either of the old women who witnessed it. They put his retirement behind the cartshed down to another reason, one which may apply to everyone, irrespective of the colour of their cloth.

When William had recovered himself, he went indoors and found Tulip in the bar, her eyes goggling with excitement. Seeing him, she turned and ran for the staircase, but he caught her easily enough on the landing, and Tulip sank in a heap on the stairs. She could not run in her English skirts; without them she could outstrip the heavy seaman as easily as a deer.

"Why did you hide behind the door?" he asked her, teasing her. She panted like a wild creature in a trap as William held her, but she did not try to escape again.

"Why did you get upset by the old parson?" asked William again.

"I don't want him to see me. Why did you drag me out of the house?" said Tulip.

She was going to have a baby in April or May; that was the reason of her ailing lately. When William heard about it he picked her up, kissed her and said: "Better two than one my lass. They will be company for each other later on."

Sambo's christening was fixed for the end of October, but when the day came William found that Tulip would not go to the church. He had not thought of this, and for sometime was puzzled to know what to do.

"You must take the child Tulip," he said, "and give him to the clergyman. It won't take long."

But Tulip only moaned, shook her head and refused again. William was not used to disobedience from her, and his face flushed with anger as he looked at the poor stubborn thing, sitting abjectly on her heels on the kitchen floor. Seeing him look so angry, with the veins swelling up on his neck, Tulip cowered away from him still more into the corner.

"Get up Tulip, stand up, go to bed," said Targett. "If you aren't well enough to attend the christening you must go to bed and stay there for the rest of the day."

She obeyed him this time, though she moved slowly and went with a sullen look on her face, hanging her head, and trailing her feet. William held back his anger while he watched her go, and did not speak again. When the time came for the christening, he changed his clothes and took Sambo up in his arms and carried him to the church himself. On the way he found plenty to show him, and to talk to him about; for first there was a goat which Sambo thought, after his father and mother, the most interesting person in the world, then when they were past the goat, there was a line of ducks walking to the stream. But going up the street William began to tell his son what kind of fish whales are, as big as ships, and in each whaler stands a harpooneer with a harpoon in his hand and lances by his side. Just at this point, they met Mr. Cronk inside the church door, and William told Sambo then that if he was a good boy he would hear the end of the story in a minute or two. When he had been christened (with Thomas Madgwick and Eglantine Clall as his godfather and his godmother) he came running back asking him: "may I kill whales now?" William paid for the christening, and laughed and said he would make him a harpooneer one day soon, and then he put five guineas in the poor box. While his father brought the newly-christened Samuel back, he told him more about the great whales off Australia, and the whaling ships, and of how, when the fish goes sounding to the bottom, the rope spins out of a wooden tub in which it is coiled, so that it smokes, and a man has to pour sea water on it out of the bailer lest it should catch fire.

When they got back home to "The Sailor's Return," young Samuel would have stayed with his father in the bar to hear more of these wonders, but Targett bid him go upstairs to his mother. The child had his father too much in awe to disobey him, but went with leaden feet lingering and looking back upon the stairs, while his mouth puckered, and when he came to his mother's room he began to weep. Tulip was lying on her bed, and was so changed by her fear that it was a wonder her own child knew her, for he had never seen her like that before, with her skin grey, her eyes rolling, her lips thrust out, and her whole face working and twitching as if she had lost her reason. On seeing her child come back to her, she seized hold of him very passionately, and then seeing that his colour was still black, she began to cry with joy. Sambo struggled with his mother, and not liking to be laid hold of he burst into tears and pushed her away and said to her:

"I want to go to Papa."

Tulip did not heed this but picked him up violently and undressed him as fast as she could with her trembling fingers, and then spent some little while looking him over to see if there were any new marks upon his body. Finding nothing she became somewhat comforted, took him into the bed with her, kissing him, and fondling him, so that at last Sambo stopped his crying and his struggling with her. To all her questions the child would only answer at cross-purposes about big fish that swam in the sea called whales, and how he was going to throw harpoons at them. Tulip kept asking him about the christening, but the child told her that the clergyman had said he would go to sea like his father and would catch whales. This puzzled his mother; she could not believe that there was anything about whales in the church, but she got nothing else out of Sambo.

Next day she asked Mrs. Clall if there were any fishermen in the church or in the Bible, and Mrs. Clall told her, yes indeed, Our Lord and the Apostles were all fishermen. There was Jonah and the whale, Tobit, the loaves and fishes, the miraculous draught of fishes, and then the clergyman were all called "fishers of souls," not to speak of the Flood and Noah's Ark.

Hearing all these mysteries explained gave Tulip the notion that now she understood the Christian religion very well, and indeed it seemed to her a reasonable and natural one for an island people, who live by fishing and sailing about the world in great ships. Even in her own country she had worshipped the sea. Later on, when she saw the font itself she became still more persuaded of the truth of her opinions concerning the Protestant religion of England as by law established.

Targett now told her that she must bestir herself, and under his direction she made a great quantity of sloe gin. This meant gathering several bushels of sloes which were then ripe and thick in all the hedgerows. When this was done, and she had sorted them out, keeping the best ones, she had to prick each one in a dozen places with a needle, and then slip them into the bottles which William had washed out and made ready. When the bottles were filled with sloes, Tulip poured in the gin, which she drew from the cask of gin in the cellar, and William drove in the corks and dipped them in a pan of melted sealing-wax, and stamped them with a seal which he had carved out beforehand in a block of lead. The device on it was a target with an arrow piercing it, with the words "Sailor's Return." This waxing and sealing the bottles was unnecessary, indeed unheard of, at this stage in the making of sloe gin. The bottles had all to be uncorked and the liquor decanted in six months' time, but the truth is that William had only just fashioned the seal and had to use it on something.

There were few incidents until Christmas came to break the monotony of the winter. William was busy serving the people who flocked to his public-house, often coming from five or six miles off, because his place was so much spoken of. "The Sailor's Return" at Maiden Newbarrow had indeed something of a name, both on account of a black woman being there, and because the new landlord had made the place so handsome, and entirely different from the miserable little pot-house which it had been for twenty years before his coming. The bleak years of the "hungry 'forties" when bad harvest had followed after bad harvest, were forgotten, and the Dorchester riots and transportations had quite gone out of men's minds. Since the end of the war the people found themselves better off than they had been since the eighteenth century, or in other words within the memory of man. Once again a labourer could eat butcher's meat at least one day a week, could drink beer, and sometimes if he liked, taste a dram of spirits. But "The Sailor's Return" would have fared badly if it had depended on labourers. Though their weak heads are the ones which get soonest fuddled, and they are the ones who stagger away from the public-house, they have only drunk a wretched three pints of small beer. Underfed labourers who work for long hours bring small profits to the publican who depends on a robuster breed of men—the farmers and the higglers of all sorts.

Whenever money passes from hand to hand in the country the innkeeper gets his fair share of it. Not a sow can be splayed, a load of straw sold for thatching, or an order for seeds placed, without going to the inn about it. This money which goes into the publican's pocket with every bargain made is money well spent, for vendor and purchaser alike are given in exchange what they most want, courage, confidence, and contentment, and if the latter is lacking, the unfortunate party can always come again and buy a golden draught of philosophy to sweeten his bad bargain. The money that goes to the inn is well spent; both sides know it, and the prosperity of our brewers and licensed houses is a fair index of the number of bargains struck in the country parts of England.

Had Maiden Newbarrow been a market town, had it even had a couple of horse-fairs in the year, or a race meeting held on High Newbarrow Down, then "The Sailor's Return" would have flourished, and Targett would have had the inn his heart desired. But Maiden Newbarrow is no more than a village, and though a certain trade is done there in sheep, wool and mutton, most of the bargains were struck in the large Dorchester bars. Still there were a certain number of glasses drunk in the parlour of "The Sailor's Return" to cement the buying and selling of sheep-dip, pigs, butter, or fleeces. In particular it was the local butchers, drovers, higglers and gypsies with ponies to sell who resorted there. Now and then came a straying sailor, taking a short cut from Poole to Weymouth or Portland, and then Targett would be sure of a long talk and a long drink himself. Sometimes he would even ask the fellow to stop the night there, and they would sit up till all hours shouting and drinking burnt brandy, all of course at William's expense. Their stories were of sailing vessels, ports, harbours, harbour-masters, new-fangled methods, Yankee clippers and the emigrant trade to Australia. It was not every stray seaman of course, who would find such a welcome waiting him. Sometimes Targett would only nod at the fellow and leave him in Tom's hands. But all the sailors who came, whatever their reception might be, would spend some little while looking over the house thoroughly, fingering the fittings Targett had put in, and admiring them silently. They were slow to take their departure, and would look round once or twice at the sign before they went away down the road, as if they were saying to themselves:

"'The Sailor's Return,' please God that I also may return and find such a house as this waiting for me."

But though he had chosen to be an innkeeper, the most sociable business which a man can undertake, where his trade must depend very much on communicating his own high spirits to his customers, thereby exciting their appetites to enjoy his other spirits, Targett was not naturally fond of company. Neither was he a man who spoke of his plans or his feelings. Thus his conversation was always about outside things, such as weather, crops, markets, news from town, maritime intelligence, and the like. This reserve or closeness of his in speech made him all the more respected in Maiden Newbarrow by those who resorted to his inn.

It was now springtime. The rains had stopped in the middle of March, the storms were over and the sun shone. Millions of flowers burst into blossom and birds into song on the same day. Tulip regained something of her natural gaiety, and went out for walks, though she was near her time. Targett, who had been drinking heavily for nearly a month, came out of the house and gazed with bloodshot eyes at the green pastures dotted with ewes and lambs. He shook himself like a spaniel coming out of the water, and called out to Tom to set open the window, then he went himself to dig the garden. The trouble that often comes between man and wife before the birth of a child had been all the worse because of the weather. Now that was changed, Targett and Tulip found themselves changed also.

And as the endless rain and slush, the falls of snow, and the thaws in February had made Targett drink, beginning in the morning and sitting all through the day in front of the fire, with a glass of whisky by his side, so the sun now made him put the bottle by. In winter the inn had been full of men, shaking off the rain from the brims of their sou'westers, or brushing the melting snow from the shoulders of their top-coats, blowing their red noses between thumb and finger, and swigging spirits till their bleary eyes watered again. Only in that way could they face the bitter east wind, the driving sleet and the long tramp home when the day's work was done, splashing through the strings of puddles, and slipping at every step in two inches of mud.

The sun shone out, the boys sang as they went to work in the morning, and everyone had a friendly greeting for his neighbour. In a week's time the road was thick with dust, and they were rolling the young wheat in the fields. Winter was forgotten, everyone was working hard with a new courage. Nobody came into the bar in the fine weather or drank spirits, only at midday the men would stop and call to Tom to bring them out a pint of ale and gulp it down quickly to quench their thirst whilst they kept their eyes fixed on the field towards which they were bound. Hedging and ditching, carting dung and spreading muck were forgotten, the cows were turned out of the stalls except at milking-time. Indoor work was over, and everyone was busy rolling, harrowing, and getting a fine tilth on the arable land to sow seeds.

In the evenings the labourers searched for peewit's eggs as they crossed the meadows on the way home; on Sunday the boys went birds' nesting. The farm-yards were full of hens with strings of chickens or ducklings just chipped out of the eggs, puppies, calves, foals and droves of newly-farrowed porkers staggered, sprawled or trotted in every direction.

Tulip gave birth to an infant daughter in the middle of April.

Mrs. Clall attended her, and William spent the day making a prawn net, not that he wanted the net but because it occupied his attention, and he could sit downstairs in the room below listening, while he was making it. For several hours there was nothing to hear except Mrs. Clall moving to and fro across the bedroom; Tulip did not cry out, or moan. But at last there was a faint cry, a whining noise, and then William ran upstairs three steps at a time, and found Mrs. Clall with a baby girl in her arms.

"Give it back to her," said he, seeing that Tulip was gazing at the child, in agony lest it should be taken away. When Tulip was given it, she smiled peacefully and soon afterwards fell asleep. The baby was a lighter colour than Sambo, a silvery grey, with staring eyes, and a thin crop of dark red curly hair, like a Rothschild lamb. Targett was not disappointed with the child, and went downstairs full of joy, and when he saw his half-finished prawn net lying on the floor laughed at himself and said aloud: "I have no use for a prawn net, God bless my heart, if ever I should have a fancy to go prawning Miller would have lent me one." Then taking it up he looked at it critically, and still laughing put it away with his gear, saying to himself:

"Well, it will come in useful next time, that is if Tulip should breed again."

When a child has been born, the whole house is usually upset, and there is a great deal of extra work. But there was less trouble with Tulip than there would have been had she been an Englishwoman. Tom

Madgwick had to light a good many fires, and boil a great many kettles, and William had to look after Sambo for most of the day, but beyond this there was no change in their lives, except that Mrs. Clall found another woman to come in one day a week to work at the wash-tub. Tulip would have got up on the second day, but Targett ordered her to stay in bed, and made her lie there a week, though it was against her wish. As soon as Tulip was up and about, she took charge of Sambo again, as well as her new baby. About a fortnight after this a parcel came addressed to Mrs. Tulip Targett. Inside there was a letter (which she would have thrown away had not William been with her) with a silver and coral rattle from Harry, and a christening mug from the rest of the family. Targett took the letter and read it aloud:

TARGETT'S FARM

MY DEAR TULIP,

We heard the good news of your having a little daughter, although William did not write as he should have done getting the good news from Lucy, who is I should say very jealous; you are a good enough Christian I know to forgive her. She has no children of her own, and that is what makes her angry. However, she has been the means of my sending this coral for the baby.

What will you call her I wonder?

The rest of the family send a silver christening mug, and you must have her christened or they will think you didn't like it. I cannot get away in this fine weather, but have hopes of seeing you in about ten days' time when we shall be less busy.

With best wishes and love to Sambo.

Hoping you and the infant are doing well,

Yours obediently,
HARRY TARGETT

This letter and the presents gave William more pleasure than he had ever expected to feel upon a like occasion. Harry he knew was friendly to him and fond of Tulip, but he would not have expected him to take the trouble to buy a present, or write a letter. Besides that, he could guess well enough what sort of letter Lucy must have written upon the occasion of the baby being born, and he knew that it was all owing to

Harry that the others had sent a christening mug. This was as good an answer to Lucy as he could wish them to make, and he laughed when he thought how angry she would be when she heard of it, as she surely would do, even if they did not tell her they had given it themselves. And Targett took the mug into the bar and showed it to the men there, and told them that his family had sent it, although he would have sworn that he did not care what any of his family thought of him, and was quite content to be a law unto himself.

Harry rode up to the inn one lovely morning in May, and arrived just as they were sitting down to the midday meal. He was singing at the top of his voice, and he went on with his song while William came to the open door. Tom ran out to take his horse, Sambo thrust his head out, peeping between his father's legs, and Tulip waved her arms wildly from the window and put her finger to her lips.

Harry finished the last bar of his song, vaulted off his horse, and shook William by the hand. "You'll have woken the baby Harry," said William laughing. "What a voice you have got. Have you fallen in love?"

Tulip came out then and Harry picked her up off the ground for a moment and said: "I saw you Tulip. But what does it matter? You see your baby isn't crying."

Tulip wriggled out of his grasp like a wild thing, half turned to run from him, but then came back, caught him by the sleeve of his coat, and drew him after her through the house into the garden where her baby was. The little creature was awake, lying on its back with wide-open grey eyes, staring at the silver rattle hanging above it.

The midday meal was just ready; Harry and Tulip came back into the kitchen. But while Tulip was beaming with the natural pride of a mother, Harry looked grave. He was thinking that he would not like his own children to be born that nasty grey colour, and that though Tulip was a good creature, William had done wrong in bringing her back with him to England, and in begetting these children that were neither one thing nor the other. But these reflections only showed themselves by a moment of thoughtfulness, and when he next spoke to Tulip it was with great tenderness and gentleness, perhaps all the more so because she looked changed to him. Her figure was no longer slim and like an arrow. Her body was heavier, he had noticed that when he lifted her. Her native grace was not yet gone; soon it would vanish, and then no one would believe that William had called her Tulip because she had seemed to him like that brilliant flower, swaying upon its slender, green, cylindrical, and sappy stalk.

Tulip was far from guessing Harry's thoughts, and they sat down gayly at the table, laughing when Harry said the baby looked as if it had been left out in the rain, and that perhaps if Sambo had been born in England he would have been paler in colour.

It did not occur to William to wonder what his brother might be thinking about him, for he never bothered himself with what other people did, or worried about questions of right and wrong. He did what he wanted to do, and never went back into the past to find anything in his life to regret, nor forward into the future to find cause for fear.

Now Harry was come they were a merry party. William called Tom to bring them a second quart of ale to take with their cheese, and while they drank it Harry told him all the news from the farm. This was principally of their sister Dolly, and of her chances of getting married.

She had had a valentine from Stevie Barnes, and had shown it to everyone. Now she was sorry she had shown it, for Stevie meant business, and Dolly could not hide her love for him any longer. It was a good match; Stevie's father was getting an old man, and Stevie would have Gibraltar Farm.

But Dolly was eaten up with vexation, just because she had begun by laughing at him, two or three Sundays ago, while the others were at church, she had asked Stevie into the house. Somehow the couple lost reckoning of the time, and when the family got back there they were sitting by the fire like man and wife. Since then Dolly had refused to see Stevie, but Harry had seen him and had told him to let her sulk. Harry then told them about Dolly's other young men, and made Tulip laugh with a story of how she had gone skating in the dark with Jem Budd. The ice had broken, since then she would never even hear of Jem without impatience.

While he was still talking about Dolly, there was a knock on the door and the postman handed in a letter for William. He took his knife and slit the seal, and cast his eye over the page. Then he stopped laughing and stared at it again. All of a sudden he jumped up from the table cursing, and started as if he would go out of the door, but stood still before he got to it as if he were dazed; then he began swearing again, so wildly, and with such filthy language that Harry thought he had gone out of his senses. Tulip also had sprung to her feet and stood watching William, ready to execute the first command which he might give her. For some moments nothing came from William's mouth but great oaths and threats, all mixed up with such a torrent of obscene words that anyone might have thought he was a mad pirate at sea.

At last however, he noticed the silent figure of Tulip standing beside him, with her eyes fixed on him questioningly, and then he turned on her, and caught hold of her, though still with the knife in his hand. But Tulip did not flinch from him as William clasped her and said: "No my girl, never fear, I shall never turn you adrift! Damn their black hearts!" and with that fell once more to cursing and swearing. A moment later he said to Harry, who was questioning him what he meant by this frenzy: "Read that! Tell me do you not smell the hand of that bitch, our own sister at Newbarrow Boys?"

Harry took the letter from him and read it over. It ran as follows:

JACOB STINGO & SONS, BREWERS & MALTSTERS STINGO'S PRIORY ALES

Confidential DORCHESTER

DEAR MR. TARGETT,

I am under the unpleasant necessity of writing to you on a private matter connected with yourself. It has been brought to my knowledge that you are living with a woman to whom you are not married—a coloured woman. Very strong representations have been made to me by respectable residents in Newbarrow and district against my continuing to let premises to a man of loose character. I may say I fully concur with this view, and should never allow any of my tenants to set a bad example in matters of Christian duty and morality to the villagers amongst whom they live. At the same time I do not wish to lose such a good tenant as you have otherwise shown yourself, and conceive that you may be able to see your error and repent of your laxity. I consider however that it is my duty to give you notice, as from next Ladyday, unless you terminate your unfortunate association with this female, and give me a positive undertaking that you will give no cause for similar scandals in the future. I am sure you will understand my position in this matter, and trust you will be able to see clearly what is not only your duty, but also so much to your interest.

Yours faithfully,
JACOB STINGO, JR.

Harry turned pale as he read the letter, and his tight lips and flashing eyes showed his indignation. But when William started again for the door, he cried out to him: "Softly William, softly, you must think over this affair before you act. Did you never plan a battle before you started fighting in Dahomey?"

"What is that?" asked William, turning round in the doorway. "Leave him to me, I will teach him to send me insolent letters."

"Wait a minute," said Harry. "If you go I will come with you, but first answer my questions William."

"Fire away then Harry; what is it you want to know?"

"Well you are not married to Tulip, are you?"

"I don't know," said William; "perhaps not in England."

"Are you married to any other woman?"

"What a question Harry!"

"Well William, you are a sailor, but you are not married to anyone else are you?"

"God help me if I am."

"You won't send Tulip away?" asked Harry. William swore by way of reply.

"Not on any account?"

"Lose Tulip for a stinking pothouse Harry? By God, do you take me for a weevil? Did you not hear me say that this inn and everything in it was bought with Tulip's pearls? Lose my Tulip who has borne me two children and who left her father's palace to wash dirty pots of beer because she loved me? Send away my Tulip? It is clear, Harry, that you have never loved a woman." Harry flushed.

"Yet you would not marry her?" he asked. William gazed at his brother as thunderstruck. "Marry her? That was not what he said. Marry her?" Then William dropped into a chair and broke into a roar of laughter that frightened Tulip more than any of his oaths. "Will that do the trick think you Harry? Well by God, we will be married today." And then William began laughing again till he sobbed. At last he was able to ask Tulip to fetch him a drink. When she had brought him a glass of beer he gulped down a mouthful, mopped his brow, and dried the tears in his eyes.

"We were married," said he, "in Dahomey, but the only one I can call a parson was a frightful fellow compared with the chap we have here. He was dressed in a royal leopard skin hung all over with the teeth of alligators, and he was a priest of the sacred python. But Tulip was given me by three women, who put her hands in mine, and told me to treat her well, to feed her and give her clothes, and to beat her when she was bad. It may not be a proper wedding here, but it took from sunrise until after midnight, and it was on a Sunday too." Then his thoughts coming back to the business in hand, William struck the table with his fist and cried out: "We will be married tomorrow. I shall go now and see the parson about it." But poor Tulip had not followed all William's talk. She had understood the oaths and the threats, and what he said about their marriage in Dahomey, all but the letter itself. And that seemed to her to have but one explanation, viz. that there was an evil spirit in it, and that some wizard or enchanter had William in his power, for in her country she had seen men and women bewitched often enough. Everything she heard him say since then made her think that she was right in her fears, and when William bellowed out that they were to be married the next day, they having been married so long already, she could not keep from bursting into sobs.

"Oh, my poor William, my dear William," said she, "some enemy has charmed you surely. Have you forgotten that we were married when I was fourteen years old, and how you had to send for me three times, at dawn, at noon, and at sunset, and then how three women of my fetish brought me to you at midnight after the feast. You spoke of the panther man; he was sacrificed at the So-sin customs for his many crimes, have you forgotten that?" Tulip uttered these words in the most desperate tones, laying hold of William as she spoke by the knees as he sat in his chair, and gazing into his eyes, while the tears streamed down her own smudge cheeks. And she shook him with all her might as if she would thereby bring him to his senses. All this caused Harry a good deal of surprise, but to William it appeared natural enough, for he understood her African superstition and understood that she had taken the letter for an enchantment.

"No, Tulip, Harry here will tell you that there is no witchcraft in this. It is only a plot to turn us out of the inn, and to defeat it you and I must be married as soon as possible—this time by a white man. Remember he did no harm to Sambo and he will do no harm either to you or me." Tulip turned to Harry, who confirmed this very solemnly, and presently succeeded in persuading her that her William was still himself, and that he had not fallen into the power of a magician.

Targett was all on fire for wedlock now, and wanted to set about it at once. He soon found however that matters of this sort cannot be settled out of hand. For when he got back from the vicarage he said sorrowfully: "Tulip and I cannot be married under the month, plague take the parson. There are a thousand things to fuss about before I can make an honest woman of her as they call it. Our banns must be read three times and that takes three Sundays."

Harry thought the sad voice in which William spoke was very comical and laughed outright. "You were always like that William," he said, "always in a hurry. You could never bear to wait for anyone. Did you never have to wait for the next tide when you were a sailor?"

"You think a deep-water sailor is the same thing as a bargeman, or a Poole harbour pilot Harry. Wait for the tide indeed! But that is waiting for God; this is waiting for a poxy parson."

The news of the marriage was soon all over the village, and the marriage became the staple of conversation until it took place. While many of the more strait-laced sort were reconciled to Targett by the news, others who were ready to tolerate sin did not rejoice to see a heathen woman married in their church, just as they had been themselves. The strongest disapproval was excited among the sinners, now that their hero Targett had had to knuckle under to parson. For look at it as they might they could find nothing to admire in his having a black wife. Mr. Cronk the clergyman was delighted; for weeks he went about with a happy face, planning how by degrees he would bring Tulip into the fold, and thus imagined himself a missionary, though one who had not to endure the hardships of a tropical climate. Young Mr. Stingo was as much surprised as he was pleased when Mr. Cronk wrote and told him of the approaching marriage, for though glad to keep his tenant he had never known that vice could get such a hold on a man as to make him marry a coloured woman rather than part from her. But the clergyman and the brewer were the only ones to be genuinely pleased by the marriage. Lucy could not believe the news, and when she arrived at the vicarage, rather red in the face from walking, and rather out of breath, and heard it confirmed, she could not hide her indignation.

"You must refuse to marry them," she said. "It is a scandal; it is an insult to me and to every respectable married woman in the parish. They are taking advantage of you Mr. Cronk. I know my brother. You must forbid the banns."

"I do not know what you mean Mrs. Sturmey," answered the clergyman. "Your brother shows a sincere desire to repair his faults in the only way possible, and I rejoice at the wedding. Remember the parable of the prodigal son, and do not show a suspicion of your brother that is beneath you."

"My brother marrying a nigger, here in this village under my eyes!" exclaimed Lucy. "I tell you he is making fun of you, of all of us, he is doing it to insult respectable people. He thinks he is doing something very clever, but it has got to be stopped."

"I fear that you misjudge your brother," said Mr. Cronk, "he is by no means a wholly bad man, only a man of bad habits. You should labour to reclaim him Mrs. Sturmey. As a Christian you must see that the only way for him to repair his error is by marrying the woman, whatever she may be on the surface."

"Fiddlesticks," said Lucy, marching to the door with her skirts rustling. "William has probably got half a dozen wives already. Marriage is the only thing that he can think of to prevent his being turned out of the inn, as he ought to be." Lucy slammed the door behind her and walked back to Newbarrow Boys.

The morning of the wedding was bright and clear, with hot sunshine. A swarm of bees came out of Mrs. Everitt's skep about eleven o'clock in the morning, and Mrs. Everitt roused the village by beating on her coal shovel with a pair of tongs. As she was fetching them the bees settled on a gooseberry bush, and drooped to the ground, but she went on beating the fireirons for half an hour, until everyone came out to look from a safe distance. She was still beating them as William with Tulip on his arm walked down the village street, and she did not stop till they had gone into the church. The sound pleased Tulip; it reminded her of the drums at her father's court. She was glad also to see that so many people had come to watch her being married, and she smiled at everyone they passed in the road. William had ordered the wedding dress from Poole, and the crinoline was so large that Tulip had only just managed to squeeze out of the door of the inn; it was an ivory silk brocade cut short three inches above Tulip's ankles showing her white silk stockings; her head was covered with a veil of real lace, her white kid gloves reached to the elbow, and it being tulip-time she carried a large bunch of scarlet tulips in her hand.

William wore a blue frock coat with a velvet collar and large brass buttons; his legs were encased in a pair of tartan trousers strapped under his boots, and his white bow tie was three times the size of any which had been seen in the neighbourhood. He carried a pair of dogskin gloves, and the ivory walking stick of a Dahomian Cabosheer, which dignity had been conferred on him by His Majesty King Gaze-oh. On his head was a large white beaver with straight sides and a very curly brim. A few yards behind the couple walked Tom Madgwick leading Sambo by one hand, while in the other he carried a large nosegay. Behind him came Mrs. Clall with the baby in her arms. The little creature was silent, but Sambo never stopped asking questions, and Tom was hard put to think of suitable replies. Everyone was waiting in the street or near the church to see them go by, and among the villagers were several people from Tarrant. But though there were a great many onlookers, and many among them nodded to Targett or touched their hats, hardly anyone came into the church to see the service. When William would have led her up the aisle, Tulip withdrew her hand from his arm and hurried to the font where she knelt for a moment or two in prayer, bowing her head to the ground. Then she rose up and scattered something into the font. Just then William came to her and after whispering a word in her ear, led her forward up the aisle.

Mr. Cronk was standing by the altar rails as this took place, and he saw nothing of what had passed, and the other persons were not yet got properly into the church so that little notice was taken of what Tulip had done. After the marriage was over, and William had signed the book in the vestry, Mrs. Clall came forward with the baby and it was christened. William gave it the name of Sheba, which he thought suitable. But it was then at the christening that Mr. Cronk saw a handful of rice in the water, some few of the grains floating, and more lying at the bottom, together with one or two shells which he believed to be water snails. On perceiving these objects he was much shocked, though not at all puzzled by how they came to be there since he assumed the rice had been thrown at the wedding, and as for the snails, he was convinced that the sexton had saved himself trouble by filling the font from the pond outside, and he determined to speak to him about it. That evening he went back to the font to take out the snails and show them to the old man, but he found that they were really bright little cowrie shells, so he put them into his waistcoat pocket and thought no more of the matter. He would never have believed it had anyone told him that a heathen sacrifice to Neptune, or Nate, the God of the Sea, had taken place in his church that morning. When the christening was over William and Tulip returned to the inn, flaunting themselves openly in their fine clothes quite as if they were the quality.

"That sailor-man thinks he can do anything because of his money," said one woman to another as they passed. "He has more money than he knows what to do with, and he throws it about shamefully. Look at what he has spent in painting that public-house. Every door and every window has had three good coats of paint since he has been in the place; and then goodness knows how much he has spent on gilding with real gold leaf on the signboard, and then that blessed weathercock of his. You would think he could find some work to do without making that there weathercock."

"Who knows how he came by all that money either. Not by honest work I'll be bound," answered another.

"And no more sense with it," replied her neighbour, "but to marry a black woman. Our English girls aren't good enough for him."

"Yes poor fellow," said Mrs. Everitt, who had just taken her swarm of bees, "I am afraid he must have picked up the habit abroad, and when once a habit gets hold of a man there is never any breaking him of it."

"If I had the breaking of him, I would soon cure him of going after a black woman," passed through the minds of the two first speakers as they gazed at Targett's handsome figure going up the street, but neither of them spoke. They were both vigorous women in the prime of life.

Tulip and William had expected Harry for the wedding. He was indeed to have been the best man. When they got back to the inn they found out what had occurred. For just as they reached the door, a dogcart drove up covered with mud, and there was Harry with Mrs. John Targett, the wife of William's elder brother, and his sister Dolly, and Francis, a boy of fourteen, who barely remembered his seafaring brother.

The party had met with an accident on the way; a train had startled the horse soon after they had crossed the railway with Dolly driving. Before Harry could take the reins they were off the road and on to the heath, and in a moment the dogcart had overturned, throwing them all into a bog-hole. No one had been hurt except Harry, who had put his thumb out of joint and was silent from pain, but the ladies' dresses were ruined; Mrs. John's temper had suffered even more than her dress, and all of the party were gloomy except the boy Francis. Dolly succeeded in appearing cheerful, for she remembered that they had come to celebrate her brother William's wedding. Poor Tulip was puzzled when Dolly threw a bag of rice, all stuck together with muddy water, into her face, but she joined in her laughter, and then Dolly gave her a squeeze (which was easier to manage than a kiss) and asked to see the baby.

Mrs. John Targett did not greet Tulip at all nor William either. As soon as she had been helped out of the dogcart she walked into the house, and made her way to the scullery, where she spent half an hour trying to wash out the stains of mud. The overturning of the dogcart had been the greatest joke that Francis had ever known in his life, he was still beside himself with joy when he thought of Mrs. John and Dolly rolling out into a mudhole in their best dresses. For some minutes after their arrival he was doubled up with laughter. At last however he was able to speak, and addressing Dolly said, pointing to Tulip: "If you only had her complexion no one would notice the mud." A moment later he asked William why he had not brought home a monkey like the uncle of a friend of his instead of. . . But at that moment Harry gave him a very hard box on the ear. The young rascal burst into tears, and went indoors to hide. Meanwhile Mrs. Clall arrived carrying little Sheba, and Tom leading Sambo. Dolly at once seized the baby, which began to cry, but her aunt was equal to her and shouted the infant down with its praises. After a few moments Mrs. Clall took it again and went into the house. Dolly then turned her attention to Sambo. The blackness of his skin took her aback even more than the blackness of his mother, but good nature triumphed. She kissed him, and the little boy grinned at her so roguishly that she could not but like him.

Harry had now unloaded the wedding presents. Chief in magnificence was a wedding cake, but unfortunately the accident had proved fatal to its beauty. The icing which should have been a field of virgin snow, was shattered into fragments, one side was flattened, and the corner was sodden with marsh water. William however declared that it would taste all the better, and carried it indoors where the others followed him, bearing other offerings. Of these the most remarkable was a present from Dolly to the bride—of a pair of black kid gloves, which might have been made from Tulip's own skin after the glow of health had left it. Harry's present was a gaudy crimson shawl, which only a gipsy woman would have worn; but he had guessed right and Tulip was delighted with it. William was so astonished at the arrival of his relations that he did not remember their wants, but Tulip who from the beginning was accustomed to social occasions such as this, ran at once into the bar, returning with a bottle of port, glasses and a corkscrew. Dolly swallowed the wine which Tulip gave her with relish, for she was tired. Tulip filled her glass again and cut her a large chunk of the wedding cake, and after filling other glasses went in search of Francis, whom she found in the bar-parlour, still whimpering from the box on his ear. She gave the boy first a glass of port and then a kiss; the wine he liked, but the kiss he wasn't sure about for he noticed a strange smell that faintly disgusted him, but increased his curiosity about her. In another minute they were good friends engaged in playing a game of bagatelle, and before they parted Tulip made him promise to pay her a visit in the summer. Left to themselves William and Dolly were soon at their ease.

"You have made this a fine place William," she said looking round her. "Did you put up that picture in wool? I made sure you did," she went on as William nodded; "you always used to have pictures of ships even before you went off to sea."

"That is the *James Baines,* and it is a good likeness of her too. She came up with us once off Cape Verde; my word she was a picture with all her canvas. No steam vessel will ever lower the record of the *James Baines:* from Liverpool to Melbourne in sixty-three days."

"I should think not," said Dolly. "Did you put those white ropes reefing back the curtains? That it like a sailor."

"Those are bo'sun's lanyards," said William. "We old fellows all get like that you may notice; we cannot help playing that we are still afloat. There's an old boy of eighty whom I know at Swanage, and his place is a museum all over. You could swear that you were in Noah's quarters in the ark."

"But you are glad to be settled now, William; you are happy, aren't you?" Dolly asked and blushed.

"Yes to be sure," said William, "I am glad to have this place for my sweet Tulip. But you would never guess what a lot of work there is to do here. And now when are you getting married Dolly?" he asked.

"I never! I suppose that devil Harry has been saying things about me." But Dolly went on at once to talk to William about her young man, a thing which she would not have done with any of the other members of her family. Between them they had finished the bottle of port when Mrs. John came in, declaring that they must start for home at once. She was tolerably free of mud now, but not in the best of tempers, and she set at once upon Dolly.

"What a sight you look dear. Gracious me! Plastered with mud like a mangold. I should think you must have had quite enough wine too," for Dolly was waving her glass in reply.

William took another bottle out of the cupboard and uncorked it, but Mrs. John firmly refused to drink.

"Now William, where is Harry? And where is Francis? Get them to put the horse in at once. We shall not be back before dark; we have had enough accidents without being benighted." Dolly was then sent off to the scullery to wash herself, and William was sent to the stables. Then Mrs. John eyed the bottle of port, eyed the wedding cake, and once more eyed the port. At the moment she looked very like a duck gecking first one way and then the other before it dare approach the morsel which has been thrown to it. Her hand was on the bottle when she heard a step, and Harry came into the room with a silly smile and his hand in bandages. He had drunk a lot of brandy to deaden the pain while Tom had been pulling at his thumb. Five minutes later Mrs. John had got the party into the dogcart and they were driving off. They had only been at "The Sailor's Return" for little over the half-hour, but not one of them was quite sober except herself. At parting they kissed Tulip with great warmth; Mrs. John was already in the dogcart. She was consoled by finding that the great cheese, which her husband had sent for William, had not been unpacked. She pushed it under her feet, and spread her skirts over it. Targett's farm was celebrated for its cheeses. They drove away; henceforward Mrs. John was in alliance with Lucy.

The day after the wedding little Sheba looked poorly; she shivered and Tulip found she would not take the breast. The child fretted all through the night, and William grumbled at the noise. "Sambo was never like that," he said. Next morning the baby was feverish, and Tulip came to William and asked him to bleed her, but this he refused to do. When he spoke however of fetching the doctor, Tulip became upset, and persuaded him that the child would be well soon, saying that all her family had been subject to agues in infancy. In the end William decided not to call the doctor, for he guessed that Tulip would be afraid of him, and he thought himself that the excitements of the wedding day might have changed Tulip's milk, and that this was the whole trouble with Sheba. It would make the matter worse he thought if Tulip were now to be frightened. Besides that, William had not a much greater opinion of the country doctors in England than of those in Africa. Two days afterwards Sheba died of pneumonia. Tulip did not cry, she walked about slowly all the next day, and did nothing. William said to her several times: "I ought to have fetched the doctor," and so Tulip came to think that the doctor had made Sheba die because they had insulted him. The second day after Sheba's death she was buried in Maiden

Newbarrow churchyard. It was a clear morning. In the elms half a dozen birds were singing; their music filled the pauses in the service. The child's parents were the only mourners, and Tulip wore the black gloves that Dolly had given her for a wedding present. When they came back from the funeral, William went to dig the garden. Sambo ran out to him and began to dig also. The sun was hot and the borders were full of flowers. When William looked up he saw a sparrow carrying a straw in its mouth being blown away by the wind. High up in the sky there were swifts wheeling. Two or three cuckoos were chasing each other in the tops of the elms. When William had dug for an hour he sent Sambo into the house to fetch him a pot of beer, and watched him bring it. The little boy's face was set in a frown: he carried the pot in both hands and staggered as he walked with his excess of care. Indoors Tulip was making the beds, she stopped for a moment and looked out of the window and saw William take the can of beer and slowly drink it nearly dry, and then bend down and give Sambo a sip. As she drew up the bedclothes she sprinkled them with tears, which made circles of moisture on the sheets, but hung in drops on the blankets. Tulip looked at them sparkling in the sun, and soon afterwards she stopped crying. When she had finished making the beds, she folded up the little blankets and quilt of the baby's cot and put them away in a drawer; then she carried the cot itself upstairs into the loft.

That evening William missed her when he came back from serving in the bar. She was nowhere in the house; he called but she did not answer. About midnight he heard the latch of the door click, and going to look, found Tulip. Seeing him she started, but as he did not seem angry she came towards him, and reached up and put her arms on his shoulders. "Come along my girl, you must turn in now," said William, but he asked her no questions as to where she had been or what she had been doing. Next morning everyone was talking of what Tulip had done that night, for it was desecration and a great scandal to the village, and saying that the vicar must punish her. She had been at the baby's grave, and had thrown away the flowers which Mrs. Clall had laid on it in the afternoon. In their place she had dug a little pit and had set in it a crock of milk, and at the foot of the grave she had put the child's rattle and one or two toys, with a little wooden horse of Sambo's, and these she had set so firmly in the earth that they were almost buried. Early in the morning the gravedigger had found them; he had broken the crock with his foot so that the milk was split on the earth, and had kicked the toys out of the ground so that they were broken. Later on a cat found a little of the milk left in the corner of the crock, and the village children saw the rattle and the broken toys. They carried them away and fought over them.

Mrs. Clall told Tom Madgwick, Tom told his master, and Targett walked down to the churchyard, where there was nothing to be seen but a smear of milk on the clay. He had expected to find more, and did not think it worth while speaking about it to Tulip, or to the clergyman.

The weather was now fine so that there was little business at the inn. William was free all day long to do what he liked, and spent most of his time working in the garden with Tulip lying near him in a chair, with her feet on the garden bench. Sambo ran between them, or dug his own little patch of garden which William had given him in one corner. The whole morning would pass away like this, and then the afternoon, without William or Tulip talking to each other; every now and then Sambo must be answered and the silence would be broken by the child's prattle and the parents' voices. Tulip watched her husband for hours as he worked. His broad back was cut by red braces, his shirt was made of that large blue and white checked material which had not yet been discarded in the navy. It was always a surprise for her to see a man so busy as William. He was a free man, yet he worked harder than an African slave. Cuckoos called, goldfinches sang in the elms, the weeks of perfect summer weather followed each other, marked only by the flowers in the garden and the dishes on the table. The first gooseberries were followed by the first peas, and they in their turn by broad beans, cherries and red currants. Only one incident occurred in six weeks, and that was no more than a fleeting glimpse of the red face and the broad back covered in black silk of Mrs. John Targett driving past in a dogcart.

William and Tulip looked after her as they came from feeding the goslings which William had just bought.

"Paying my sister Lucy a visit!" he said.

"Will she come here afterwards?" asked Tulip.

"Not much chance of that."

"I hope she keeps on that tack always," said Tulip smiling. "But who was driving? It was not Harry."

"That must be her nephew, Charlie Tizard."

Two or three days after this William received a letter from Harry. It ran as follows:

Targett's Farm

Dear William,

I am writing to say you may expect me on Tuesday next week, as I wish to pay you and Tulip a farewell visit before I leave England. If I know your mind, we think alike about farming and it being no life for a young man. I, a younger son, cannot ever expect a farm of my own. Never to marry, and to live on a labourer's wages all my life is my inheritance and prospects. I therefore sail Saturday following for New Orleans, and fancy that in a few months I shall be fighting Indians and killing buffaloes with the best of them,

Your affectionate brother,
Harry Targett

William read it aloud to Tulip, who was so dismayed at the thought of losing Harry that her eyes filled with tears, but William told her that there was no cause to weep, that Harry was doing the right thing in going, and that she must make young Francis take his place.

"I shall give him a hundred pounds to start with," he declared. "Harry cannot have a penny of his own except what John gives him. I wonder that he has saved his passage money. He is quite right; a farmer never sees anything of the world beyond the nearest market town. Harry is too much of a man to live by scraping dung out of a yard. He aspires to fortune, as I have done myself in my time. I shouldn't have found you if I had not run off to sea."

When Harry came he did not show much of this fire and dash. He was paler than usual, and confessed that he was distressed at his departure. However there was no talk of turning back now that he had said good-bye to all his friends round Targett's Farm. It was late when he arrived, and after a scanty supper, he retired to bed. Next morning Tulip found herself alone with him, and after breakfast asked him had he no girl he was sorry to leave behind.

That made him laugh, and he answered her: "No one as much as you dear Tulip." He was going to kiss her then, but seeing her still serious, and gazing into his eyes with a look of grave enquiry, he became rather shame-faced, and said: "It is because of the girls I am going Tulip. There have been half a dozen or so; I cannot marry and now the country is too hot to hold me." He sighed then smiled, and added: "I shall be forgotten in three months," and sighed again. "Never mind," said Tulip, "you are not going to be a sailor, you will find plenty of girls in America." Harry laughed at this, and told her she was the best creature in the world. Her simple words comforted him.

In the afternoon William drove Tulip and Harry to the sea, and took them out sailing. Directly they were on board he began talking about America and the Americans, and of what Harry would find when he had crossed the ocean. But Harry did not enjoy the motion of the boat, and could not pay very much attention to what William was saying. Very soon he felt that he hated America, and that perhaps it would be better to enlist in the army. But then he reflected that he had already paid his passage money, and that there was no escaping doing what he had planned for so long, and looked forward to so much and which now seemed to him to be the worst thing he could have chosen. Meanwhile William was telling him that he ought to settle somewhere near York River and grow tobacco. Very soon he went on to talk about shipbuilding, and how the Yankees had captured the Australian emigrant trade with their clippers, until we had got it back by buying American built ships like the *James Baines* and the *Lightening,* and that soon we should be building fast clippers ourselves.

As they were driving home Tulip asked suddenly: "What colour are the girls in America William?" Both the brothers laughed at this question, and William told her that they were of all colours, and that the negroes were slaves from Dahomey, and all along the coast, who had been sold to the plantations. "Oh that riff-raff," said Tulip. "My family has sold thousands of them every year. They are all wretches who ought to have been killed at the annual customs, but my ancestors the kings of Dahomey have always been very kind men, and have always spared as many lives as they could, and sold the wretches off to the white men at Whydah. You will not find the kind of girl you want among people like that." She was so earnest on this subject that Harry at last promised her that he would never marry a black girl though she could not understand why the two men laughed at her. That evening William mixed a big bowl of cold punch; Tulip alternately played on her little pipe, and danced, and both the brothers sang. By midnight Harry had got thoroughly drunk. As he was trying to dance he slipped on the floor. Then sitting up he said to William: "I love your little black girl, I swear I do. She is a dear creature, but you know William, you should not have brought her to England. You should not William, because you see she is black. You should not forget that because you ought not to mix the two breeds." William laughed at this. "Wait till you have married the King of Spain's daughter Harry, then you can talk. Now it is time for you to come along to bed." But Harry would not go to bed until Tulip had kissed him, had told him that she loved him, and promised that she bore no malice for what he had said, which she did very readily because she had not overheard his words. Next day Tom harnessed the dogcart and William and Harry drove off. William was going with his brother all the way to Southampton. It would do him good, he said, to go aboard a ship once more. In his pocket he put the bag in which he kept all his money. He had not yet spoken to Harry of what he was going to give him, and indeed had not decided in his own mind how much he could spare him.

The day after the departure of Harry and William, Tulip dressed herself in her best clothes, viz. those she had worn at her wedding, except that on this occasion she wore a poke bonnet of cream-coloured straw, with a scarlet riband instead of a veil. There was no kind of occasion for this fine raiment which she put on only because there was no one whose opinion she valued to see her, and because she wanted to wear her wedding dress twice. In the matter of the love of fine clothes there was very little difference between Tulip and any grand lady in London. While she dressed herself thus, she thought of how her sisters would crowd about her if they could see her in these English clothes. What questions they would ask her! What fun they would all have together if she were at home even if it were only for an hour!

Her life here, so she said to herself, was only William and Sambo, and the memory of little Sheba, and nothing outside. She did not regret it, yet she missed the crowds, the constant stream of people, and the continual excitement of the palace. And more than all she missed the ceremonies, the colour, the military reviews, and the dances far into the night. Thinking of this, Tulip saw again in her mind's eye the great open square in front of the Komasi palace, a space of beaten red clay, the ochreous dust lying thick on the ground, the sun blazing, a crowd gathered to watch, the little boys darting naked here and there, and then the shuffle of the soldiers in their blue uniforms with white sashes and white fillets, and the banging of the drums. In front marched the terrible razor women with skulls hanging at their girdles. All that was over. Never again would she hear the cymbals and the drums. How they had rolled and throbbed and filled the whole town so that even the earth had trembled! How she had danced to that music on the hot sulphurous nights!

Tulip called Sambo and giving him a toy to carry, a present for his little dead sister, she set off with him, and together they sauntered through the village street to the churchyard. As Tulip looked about her at the green landscape of the English country her mind was busy with memories, and she could not help comparing the place where she had been brought up and the place where she was now living. It seemed to her that the white people here, although they could do so much, did not know how to live; that their lives were like the lives of animals and not like those of human beings. They went out all day into the fields like the cows going out to graze; when they came back at night they chewed the cud like cows, and if they talked at all talked slowly and awkwardly. They seemed always to be asleep, and even in their moments of ill-temper they did not wake up. Then Tulip began to imagine a mixed world, half Africa and half England. If a dozen drums with pipes, cymbals, and rattles were set on the village green, would that bring the people out to dance? Tulip laughed aloud at the incongruity of such people dancing to proper music; then she thought of the labourers' soiled corduroy trousers and their huge hobnailed boots, and she was silent with disgust. She entered the churchyard, and told Sambo to thrust the doll he was carrying into the little mound of Sheba's grave. They did not linger in a place where so many ghosts of strange people were likely to be met with. Near to the church there was a farm with its yard shut from the road by a high stone wall.

While she was loitering beneath this wall, Tulip heard a sudden sound in the road and saw a forkful of cowdung, together with something bloody and very filthy, lying in front of her in the road at her feet. She looked up at once and caught sight of the tip of a boy's nose, and then had just time to take a step backwards and so dodge another forkfull of filth. There were whispers on the other side of the wall, and she heard the words: "Come on quick, turn old Jemmy loose on her," and then there was the sound of boys running away across the yard. One or two specks of filth had fallen on Tulip's sleeve. She stopped and cleaned them off as best she could with a handful of leaves. The entrance of the farmyard was some little way down the road. Just before Tulip got abreast of it, she heard boys shouting, the banging of a stick on the wooden doors of the shed, and the sound of a beast rushing to and fro. The next moment a red bull ran out into the road and, pulling up short, slipped down. When the brute got up he looked about him, glowered at Tulip and Sambo, shook his head and bellowed. Tulip noticed how dusty the bull's coat was, straws were clinging to him, and on his withers there was a dark patch stained with damp. She bent down and picked Sambo up in her arms. While she was stooping, two boys and a young man rushed out after the bull, and threw stones. One of these stones struck Tulip on the temple. Still gripping Sambo in her left hand, she stooped to pick up the stone. Her head swam, for a moment she fumbled; the blood was running down the side of her cheek. Then she grasped the stone—it was a large yellow flint—and she looked up. The bull was moving towards her; Tulip yelled, and still holding Sambo under her arm, ran straight at him, screaming at the top of her voice. Just before she reached him, the bull turned broadside on to her, and looking at her out of one eye, broke into a gallop and nearly knocking down one of the boys disappeared into the yard. Tulip stopped, and at once Sambo began howling at the top of his voice. Facing her she saw a young man holding a prong. Tulip raised her arm with the stone in her hand, but she did not throw it.

"Tamuley, Tamuley," screamed Tulip. The young man looked at her uneasily.

"I ain't afraid of you," he said shifting his feet. "I ain't done nothing to you. I didn't know you were there."

Tulip screamed at him again in the Ffon gibberish of her own country; her face was covered with blood, and it was this blood which set Sambo screaming. Tulip still waved the stone round her head, and the young man slowly walked back to the yard gate. Tulip now turned her attention to Sambo, and tried to still his cries. When she had got a little way down the road there were loud guffaws of laughter behind her. At home Tulip washed away the blood, and found a deep cut on the top of her temple in the wool, but it did not hurt her very much, or for very long. The bloodstains and spatters of dung on her wedding dress seemed to her much more serious, but they were all got rid of with long soaking in cold water.

After this Tulip kept close about the inn, but she did not escape persecution. Once, Tom being absent for a minute, she went into the bar to serve a carter. Seeing her, he swore and made as if to go for her. This time Tulip was able to turn the tables, for she first dashed a pint of beer into his face, and then taking sure aim, threw the tankard after it, cutting him on the bridge of the nose. The carter beat a retreat into the open air, and Tulip ran out the opposite way into the garden. This incident roused up a greater hostility against her than there had ever been before; boys haunted the garden hedges in order to throw stones at her and Sambo, and friends of the carter shouted out abuse of her whenever they came near to the inn. Poor Tom Madgwick found this very alarming, he was never easy unless he were close at hand, and he begged Tulip everyday to keep within doors, if only for his peace of mind, and in his anxiety he carried buckets of water upstairs in case of fire. What is more he kept the shot-gun loaded under the counter of the bar, in case the worst should happen. Mrs. Clall was even more upset than Tom, which came from her living in the village. But her feeling was not terror, she did not look for any mischief to be done, but was full of shame to be seen going to work at the inn. It is true that she loved Sambo and respected Tulip, and felt pity for her, but she got so much abuse from the old women her neighbours, that she declared that she was ill and took to her bed so as to stop away. This weakness of hers had one excellent result, it kept Tulip busy in the house, so that she was not always fretting to go outdoors.

William though expected everyday, did not return.

Tulip was not one soon to become uneasy. She was inured to a life full of dangers and of accidents, and a few days' delay on a journey was nothing strange to her. Moreover she had the greatest confidence in William and knew he could take care of himself very well. Yet, as he had been absent now for a week, she began to wonder, and unconsciously to look out for him.

When William had been gone ten days and Tulip and Tom had been left more and more alone, and cut off from the village, Tulip heard a knock at the door and went to open it. A visitor was a rare thing now at the inn, for only one or two labourers, and the blacksmith and his mate, still frequented the bar in the evening. In the middle of the day a farmer or a higgler would sometimes come and drink a glass. Such men of course were above the opinion of the village people; the others, who were hardened drinkers, were indifferent to it or below it.

On the doorstep was a lady whom Tulip at once guessed was William's sister, for she had the same open-hearted face and splendid figure, and when she spoke Tulip was sure of the relationship, for she had the soft burring voice of all the Targetts, only her eyes were different, small eyes with a greedy look in them.

Though she was standing below Tulip on the step, she rose a head above her, and her rich dress with its full crinoline filled the narrow doorway of the inn.

"May I come in?" she asked.

"I think that you must be Mrs. Sturmey," said Tulip.

"Yes, I am William's sister. I have long wanted to have a look at you, not that I ever expected to pay you a visit since I do not approve of William's bringing you here, or of his marrying you."

"Will you come in all the same, please?" said Tulip.

Mrs. Sturmey entered, and her small eyes flitted over the things that she saw, sorting them immediately into two classes; those she would like for herself and those she would not.

"I see you have a parrot," she said. "Did you bring that with you?" At her look the bird began its slow, uneasy dance.

"William had it before I knew him," said Tulip. "He brought it back from Brazil." And at these words Lucy said to herself that the least William could have done was to bring her a parrot, but then of course William had no family feeling. A moment afterwards Sambo came into the room, but his aunt at once placed him in the second class, among the undesirables. She asked his age, while the little boy gazed at her with perfect composure.

"He is three years old," said Tulip. "He will be four next October."

"I suppose you both find the climate very trying after Africa," said Mrs. Sturmey. "They say the change of air makes children very delicate."

Tulip silently cut a piece of cake and poured out a glass of sherry, but her sister-in-law refused any refreshment.

"How long is it then that you have known William?" she asked. "Not long before you left Africa, I suppose?"

Tulip counted on her fingers. "We have been married five years now," she answered. "But I saw William six months before I married him, on his first visit to Abomey."

Mrs. Sturmey seemed greatly surprised at this information, and without saying anything she silently looked several times first at Sambo and then at his mother.

"You know the village people do not like William having a black wife with a black child," she said at last. "They think it very wrong just as I do."

At these words Tulip's whole face shone with delight and her teeth flashed as she smiled broadly.

"Well there is very strong feeling against William," Lucy went on. "The men will not come to the public-house, and they threaten to do all sorts of things, though only behind his back of course."

"William can lick all that trash," said Tulip.

“Perhaps he might,” answered Lucy, “Of course one need not pay attention to what the labourers say, but William has gone away, and it is not very safe for you. Mr. Sturmey and I both think that you and the little boy ought to go back to wherever you came from.”

“My country is far away, and here even the name of our king is unknown,” said Tulip.

“If anything happens to you I know that William will lay it at our door, which would be most unjust,” said Lucy. “It is all his fault for bringing you here. But he will say that it is because we did not accept you as part of the family. But where is William?”

Tulip’s face showed plainly that she could not answer this question, only after a minute she said: “William is all right. I do not worry about him.”

“Suppose he has deserted you,” said Lucy. “What will happen then? I think that he sees that he made a mistake, and that it would be better for you to go away for your own sake and for the sake of the little boy. William is quite untrustworthy. He did not tell anybody the first time that he went off to sea, and left everything to my brother John in the most heartless way. I don’t think that you will see William again and the best thing for you is to go and live at Dorchester for a time; then if William does not come back you should go on to Southampton or Bristol.”

“I shall wait here,” said Tulip. “You cannot frighten a black girl like me; I have seen a lot of worse people than any of you are here.”

Lucy looked at her sister-in-law gently, for much as she disliked her existence she approved her spirit.

“You know that I do not like you,” she said. “For you can never be one of us, but I came here today to see if my husband and I can do anything to help you. William has never done anything for us, but that does not affect what is my duty. I have spoken about you to Mr. Cronk, and he agrees that you will never be happy here, and that the little boy ought not to live here. They say native children never do well in England. When you come to me for help you shall have it, for no doubt William has taken all the money with him.”

Tulip, who had been watching her visitor with a puzzled expression, rose at these words and left the room, returning directly afterwards with a purse.

“Will you pray for me?” she asked, and giving a meaning smile put the purse into her sister-in-law’s hand. “Please pray for me.”

"Of course I shall. I always do pray for you," said Lucy.

"Different prayers now," said Tulip.

"What are you giving me this money for? Do you want me to take care of it for you?" asked Lucy.

"Yes."

"Very well. You ought to leave the village at once," said Lucy.

"Not till you have prayed, with good prayers for me and Sambo."

Tulip regained her composure as Mrs. Sturmey stowed away the purse in her pocket. She had been frightened, but now as she accompanied her sister-in-law to the front door she smiled cynically.

"People are much the same the whole world over," she thought. Often and again she had seen her father paying money to a witch or a wizard! Once they had taken money they were powerless for two or three months to do any harm. Lucy, she thought, was well worth any money. After she had shut the door, Tulip danced down the passage in triumph.

All her African experience had taught her that witches do not visit one when they mean mischief. Now that Lucy was paid no doubt the village people would behave better to her, and would not frighten Sambo anymore.

Tulip was surprised when the next day two or three men shouted threateningly at the inn, as they were passing on their way back home from work.

Targett came back after an absence of three weeks.

It was close on midnight when Tulip was woken up by hearing a man moving in the house. She got out of bed, and taking William's cutlass in her hand, went downstairs, moving very softly for she thought it was some man come from the village, that had broken in to rob or maybe to murder her. There was a light in the dining-room, so she threw open the door, lifting up the point of the cutlass as she did so. William was sitting taking off his boots.

"Why Tulip, how you did startle me," he said, and getting up from his seat, took her in his arms. "Who were you expecting lass, with that cutlass? You should have woken Tom."

"Are you alone?" asked Tulip.

"Yes, who should I have with me? I am glad to be back."

By the light of the candle Tulip saw that William had a black eye and a cut lip. His fine coat was gone; in its place was a seaman's jersey. He was dirty and unshaven. He looked thinner and more vigorous than when he had left.

"Is there any food in the house?" he asked. Tulip brought a ham, a loaf of bread, cheese and a bottle of sherry.

As William carved the ham, Tulip saw his hands were trembling with hunger. He took a few mouthfuls at once. Tulip drew the cork from the bottle and poured him out a glass of wine. At the taste of it, William sighed and lay back in his chair. He ate silently, only interrupting himself to say: "Cut some more of the ham. I shall be ready for it as fast as you cut it."

At last he stopped her and began eating cheese. Tulip waited silently. When he had finished she brought the decanter of brandy and William's slippers and filled his pipe.

"No thanks Tulip. I'll turn in now."

Before he went to sleep he asked: "How's Sambo?" Then he added "I went to Goodwood—to the races. And there I was robbed."

Next morning William went into the bar before breakfast to speak with Tom and ask him how trade had been going in his absence. While he was talking with him Tulip went out in front of the house to let out the geese. As she and Sambo were watching the birds, she saw a waggon that was passing along the road draw up and the men with it stop and look at her. But now that William was back she felt secure, and so she did not retreat indoors as she might otherwise have done.

Just then Tom was saying that he had been anxious ever since they had set on Mrs. Tulip in the village, and that since people had turned so very disobliging he had kept the gun loaded behind the bar.

William had not heard a word of this from Tulip, so he questioned Tom very particularly and got the whole story from him. Now that he heard it William understood better what had led Tulip to bring down his cutlass with her the night before, unsheathed and naked in her hand, but this was only another example of what he was familiar with already from numberless incidents in Africa—that is Tulip's courage. Such boldness was nothing like so surprising as it would have been in a white woman. While William was talking with Tom he heard a shouting outside, with several great oaths, and the words: "Drown the little bastard in the stream Jemmy. We won't have them here breeding black babies in England." Then came the crack of a whip and a howl from Sambo.

William ran to the door and saw that a carter was standing near Tulip flourishing his whip, while his boy was dragging Sambo along by the hair towards the brook. But directly William came out the fellow dropped the whip and ran, while his boy let go of Sambo and trying to jump the brook, missed his footing and fell in on his knees, though he picked himself up and scrambled out the other side, and so made good his escape with only a wetting. Seeing the carter run so earnestly William did not chase the man, but went up to Tulip, who was drying Sambo's tears, and put his arm round her and told her that her tormentors would soon learn that he was back, and that he would not leave her again on any account, and bid her have no fear. But Tulip was not hurt, nor much distressed, for the carter, who was the man whose nose she had broken with the pint pot, had not used his whip on her, and she had stood still, knowing that William was at hand. Finding no mischief had been done William picked up the carter's great whip, all bound round with two or three score brass rings. He cracked it once or twice; then he noticed the team of horses and loaded waggon standing in the roadway near by.

The carter and his boy were out of sight now, so William smiled to himself and turned the leaders' head towards the inn, and drew the waggon out of the road, just outside his own doorway. Then he told Tom to give each horse its nosebag, and to chain the wheels and went himself in to breakfast, laughing at the fix in which the carter had got himself. After breakfast William spent sometime washing himself and shaving, and then got Tulip to cut his hair, and every now and then gave a glance out of the window at the waggon, but there was still no sign of the carter. It was just before midday, and the horses were still standing patiently, when William saw a rough-looking customer coming to the inn. He was a stout fellow with a body round as a barrel, with a very red face, a cauliflower ear, and a coloured handkerchief knotted round his throat.

William went out to the doorstep and asked him: "Have you come to fetch away the team?"

"Not that I know of," answered the man. "I came for a quart of ale, but if you want them taken anywhere, I'll do the job."

"No, someone will come along presently, and it is no business of mine," answered Targett, and he went indoors and drew the customer his beer.

When he had taken a swig at it the fellow asked William if any of the neighbouring farmers were short of hands, for he was in need of a job. Then he added: "I'm a pug by rights and one who has earned good money in the ring."

The word *earned* seemed to take his fancy, for he repeated it several times with various oaths. "I believe you," said William with an amused glance at the man's ear. "You look as if you had earned it."

"When I was a youngster," the prizefighter went on, "the purses were smaller and the men bigger. Why you can see men today fighting for fifty pounds a side that would never have been allowed in the ring fifteen years ago. Look at Sayers! Tom Sayers champion of the world! At ten stone! For why I ask you? Because there isn't a heavy-weight in England that can box!"

The prize ring and everything relating to it was a topic in which William took great interest, so that now he drew himself a glass of beer and prepared to listen, while the stranger continued after lowering his voice to a whisper.

"Someone has put it round that I'm too old. I want to find that fellow. I'll twist his liver. Too old! There's a very big surprise coming for some of them this winter when I get in the ring again."

"That's right," said William. "That's the spirit that wins many a fight. No man is beaten till he thinks he is."

"That's God's truth," said the boxer. "But Harry Broome there at the 'Albion' in Portsmouth, he was champion himself for a bit like his brother Johnny, he wouldn't put up ten quid for me, the dirty Brum! 'It's no use Jack,' he said to me, 'you'll never see the inside of a ring again. Any good sailor boy of twenty is worth more to me than you are.' I'll teach his young cocks to fight! Why I've lived all my life in Portsmouth and I've never met the sailor yet who could stand up to me for twenty rounds."

Targett laughed at this. "I am a sailor myself," he said. "I might take you at your word you know."

The pugilist drank off his beer and looked Targett up and down with a crafty eye, but a fight there and then offered him no attractions.

"I'm not saying anything against sailors Mister, but things aren't what they were, nor yet what they ought to be in England."

"That's right," said William and drawing the man another pint he told him to have a drink at his expense for he loved the noble science which he had often heard had made England what she was, and which distinguished Britons from every kind of foreigner.

The boxer swore that William was a gentleman, and at once continued his story.

"Seeing Harry Broome would not have me, the damned flashy Brum, I walked to London, and went into Alec Keane's house, the 'Three Tuns' in Moor Street. Now Alec used to be the finest sportsman in England; anyone will tell you that he has done more for the ring than any licensed gentleman living; but Alec just said to me: 'Jack old friend, I've got my hands full with a nigger-boy, and I've no money to spare for you though you look fine.' A British sportsman backing a bloody black man and letting Jack Sait starve! It isn't right."

William would have interrupted his visitor, but the fellow went on: "And then there are the Sheenies. They are taking up the game now they see that there is money in it; but they can't box, they only bite and butt and use the spikes on their boots."

"You must expect to fight all comers," said William. "And I have known niggers who could stand up to any man, and who would fight as fair as you could wish."

Just then Mr. Molten a farmer from Tarrant entered the bar and said: "I've come for my team and my waggon Mr. Targett, and I don't advise you to try any of your nonsense with me."

"I am glad that you have stepped round Sir," answered William. "I was saying to my man Tom just now that there ought to be a pound in the village where we could put your horses. Your man ran off like a hare; I don't know where he will have got to by now unless he has enlisted himself in the army, but he has so little stomach for fighting that I should not think that they would keep him long."

"There was a whip too," said the farmer.

"I am keeping the whip," said William. "If you ever do see that carter of yours again tell him that I am keeping it on purpose for him." Then William picked up the whip and going out to where the team was standing he amused himself for some moments by cracking it, so that the horses fidgetted.

"Come on now both of you," cried the prizefighter. "Put up your mauleys and the best man shall have the whip. I love a fight and I will see fair play."

But the farmer was already turning his horses round, and affected not to hear when William laughed and said:

"I think I can keep the whip without fighting any of our dungyard bumpkins." Then as the farmer was getting into his waggon he called out to him: "This bloodthirsty chap here wants a job. You might take him on as your new carter. He is an old prizefighter he tells me."

"I don't want any new carter," grumbled the farmer, who resented Targett's way of chaffing him. "And I don't need any of your advice, Mr. Targett."

Then he turned round on the edge of the waggon, scratched his head, and added: "A prizefighter is he? Well, maybe I can find a job for him then if he'll come along of me, and if he's willing."

Jack Sait did not need telling twice and scrambled over the tail-board of the waggon; the farmer struck the horses a blow with the doubled reins and they moved off.

That evening the bar was full. Many of the old customers were back in their places. William did not serve, but leaned over the bar in his fine clothes, smoking a pipe. He scarcely spoke; if addressed, he nodded his head, or took the pipe from his mouth and blew out a puff of smoke or spat. There was nothing new in all this for William. It had been just the same thing before, often enough, when he had dealt with an unruly crew; in every latitude men are the same. William did not despise them for fawning on him now that he had come back to the village. He did not think it strange that they should flock good-temperedly to drink, underneath the very whip with which he had threatened one of their mates. Indeed had the carter come in to ask him for a glass of beer in the evening, though he had run from him that morning, the only thing that would have surprised William was that he should have got over his fear, and be ready to stand the chaff of the others. William expected to be stood a drink by that carter before many weeks were out.

Now and then the beaming face of black Tulip was thrust through a hatchway at the back of the bar. She never looked in without a reasonable excuse.

"Tom, here is the corkscrew," she would say on one occasion, on the next reprove him for using a dirty cloth on the glasses, and hand him a clean one. At last she could restrain herself no longer and she walked into the bar crowded with men, the very men who had been threatening or shouting at her for the three weeks past whenever they had caught sight of her.

"Are you going to sit up for the gentleman who left his whip behind him?" she asked in a ringing insolent voice.

Then she tossed her head, and without glancing to right or left, without looking at any of the men in the bar, swaggered to the door. "Don't chase anymore of them William," she said, "or we shall lose all our trade." She slammed the door after her as the men roared at this sally.

William knocked out his pipe. "I'll say goodnight then, for fear I should get into more mischief. Tom will look after you gentlemen."

But although William had achieved a triumph that day, his difficulties were not yet over. His horse and trap had disappeared on his excursion to Goodwood, together with his rings, his watch and chain and his best suit of clothes. Next day he asked Tom Madgwick for the sum of money he had left in his hands while he was away.

"Mrs. Tulip has had it Sir," said Tom.

William asked Tulip what she had done with the money. For the first minute she did not understand. Then she put her finger on her lips and whispered: "I gave it all to the witch, to buy prayers from her."

"To the parson?" asked William scornfully.

"No to your sister. She was full of mischief when she came here, but I gave her that money, and now she won't do us any harm."

At first William could make nothing of what poor deluded Tulip told him, but he showed very plainly his relief that the money had gone to one of his own family. "Well, I must get the money back. I will send Tom round to the farm with a note."

"No William, please do not do that. It will mean that she will do great harm to us. She came to threaten me. Tell me, did you not have bad luck while you were away? That was Lucy's doing. If I had not paid that money you might never have come back. She threatened Sambo also."

The idea of his sister having strange powers amused William, and he could not help grinning as Tulip spoke. Perhaps if Lucy had not been his sister but an African, and if all this had taken place in Dahomey and not in Dorset, he would have been less sceptical. However his curiosity was awakened, for he felt sure that Lucy must have come with some purpose, and that the last thing she could have intended was to work on Tulip's fears in order to extract money from her. "What did Lucy say when she came?" he asked. Tulip pouted. "She said that I must go away to Africa and that I must take Sambo away from here, and that I had done you a great deal of harm. She said you would never come back while I was still here. . ." Tulip burst into tears. She could not tell William that Lucy had said he had deserted her and gone to America with Harry. William picked her up in his arms, and sat down in the high-backed chair with her on his knee. "What else did she say?"

"She said that Sambo would die as she had made our little Sheba die."

"Did she say why she had come?"

"She came to get the money," said Tulip. "I am not stupid about those witch-people William. You know yourself how they used to come to my father and tell him all sorts of dreadful things:—that it would not rain for a year; that it would not stop raining for a year; that the cattle would all die; that leopards would kill all the women who were with child. My father used to listen to them, just as I listened to Lucy, and then get up without saying anything, and go to his treasury, and come back with a rich present. Then the witch would go away, and nothing like he had described would come to pass. But if my father had been a mean man, if he had loved his treasure better than his people, they would have all died of hunger or thirst and there would have been no children born that year, except in the royal houses."

"What did Lucy say when you gave her the money?"

"She said she would take care of me now."

William wrote a note, and sent it to Lucy's husband by Tom Madgwick telling him to wait for an answer. It ran as follows:

"The Sailor's Return"

Sir,

I beg to inform you that while I was away your wife, and my sister, called here without my permission and took away the sum of seventeen pounds.

Please hand it to bearer, who has my authority to receive it, and who will give you a written receipt for it. I shall take no further proceedings in the matter after you have refunded the amount.

Yours obediently,
William Targett

Tom was a long time gone. When he was back he handed William a small canvas bag with money, and told him that the letter which he had delivered had thrown them into a very great disturbance at Newbarrow Boys. Mr. Sturmey had read it before Tom, his face had flushed, and he had gone off, calling for his wife and saying: "What's this, what's this, money and kept secret?" High words had followed between husband and wife, who were wrangling for an hour before Mr. Sturmey came out again with the bag of money, and asked Tom for a receipt. The return of this money was fortunate, for now William could pay what was owing to the brewer, and see his way clear for another month more. To get some more in hand, William decided to sell Tulip's trinkets and rings, and in that way he thought he could tide over until the winter.

Then he had another chance of bringing his ship into port, or so he thought. That was that he knew the name of a horse which he believed would win the St. Leger, for William had always had great belief in his own luck.

Tulip could now go out again in safety, but she did not venture far, for she feared Lucy, and though she did not dare argue with William anymore, she was full of terror now that he had got back the money which she thought she had spent so well. When William asked her for the necklace of brilliants he had given her, and for her gold bangles and her rings, she ran to fetch them with a merry face, and gave him all, not keeping one thing back. Then putting her arms round his neck, she begged him to give them all to Lucy, or to some powerful wizard who could protect them against her.

Next morning Francis Targett, who had ridden over on his pony, arrived on his promised visit, in a high state of excitement and delight as he was to stay two or three days and he had never slept away from home before.

Early in the afternoon Tulip, Francis and Sambo, taking baskets with them, went out into the fields to gather mushrooms. The sun was hot, and when they had got as many of the buttons as would make a jar of catsup they sat down, and Francis asking first one question and then another about Africa, led Tulip on to tell him something of the history of her country while Sambo ran up and down over the turf chasing the little blue butterflies and the meadow browns.

"The first of our kings in the written history," she began, "was Agarjah the Great. There is not much to tell about him except that he defeated everyone, and he was the first to raise an army of women and so make Dahomey into the greatest kingdom in Africa. The names of many of the peoples whom he conquered are now unknown, for he left no living creature behind him where his armies had passed. But among the peoples whom he conquered and who still exist are the Jackins, the Tuffos, the Mackies, and until recently the Oyos. He captured Save the chief town of the Whydahs; then he raided the coast towns, defeated the Dutch, looted the white men's factories, and took many of them prisoners but pardoned them. When the English Governor took part against him, he had him killed. The second king was Boss Hardy, a wicked man and a bad king. When his father died he drowned his elder brother Zinga in the sea, because he knew that it was not lawful to shed the royal blood. Very soon trouble came on him to punish him for this, for it does not do to obey the laws only by words and to disobey what the words mean. The Mew with half the army. . ."

"What is the Mew?" asked Francis interrupting her.

"The Mew is the second general who commands the left wing of the army," answered Tulip. "Over him there is the Gaw, who is the chief general. The Mew revolted, but the Gaw defeated him. But perhaps this does not interest you? It is a lesson which I used to learn when I was a little girl. Would you rather that I talked to you about elephants?"

"No, go on, tell me about the Mew," said Francis.

"I have told you—the Gaw defeated the Mew. Then the Oyos attacked the king, who ran away and hid in the English fort at Whydah with Mr. Gregory while they burnt Abomey and Kana shouting with joy. After that Boss Hardy had to pay tribute to the Oyos every year, which continued as a drain and a dishonour to our country until my father defeated and utterly subdued them and enlisted the surviving Oyos in his army. Boss Hardy then became afraid of the Whydahs, and persuaded a prince of that country to follow his own evil example, for in that way he hoped that the Whydahs would be punished as he had been himself. This young man killed his elder brother the king, and ate his heart, and not long afterwards became white with leprosy and died miserably. After his death, while the old Gaw was away fighting, the Whydahs attacked Whydah, which had always been an object of their desire. They captured the town and slew the viceroy, but when the Gaw returned they were easily driven out again with great slaughter. Boss Hardy then made one named Tanga viceroy of Whydah. He was not an entire man, but a gelded creature taken from the women's quarters in the Royal Palace. In spite of that, when he was made viceroy he would not be contented with less than two hundred wives, buying all the most beautiful girls up and down the coast. He was not jealous though, for he amused himself by watching their pleasures with his guests whom he invited to his palace for that purpose, and if there was ever any dispute among the women, Tanga judged between them. After a time this strange creature having risen so high as to be viceroy, fancied that he would make himself king, not that he could hope to found a dynasty. The first thing that he did was to attack the Englishman, Gregory, in his fort, but in this he was unsuccessful, and while he wasted his time there, messengers ran to warn Boss Hardy of Tanga's treachery. The king at once sent an army to Whydah and Tanga shut himself up in his palace, with his wives and all his friends. Then before his eyes, all that crew of men and women cut each other's throats until only Tanga was left alive; he ran out of his palace and a woman shot him as he came down the steps. When they looked inside the doors they saw a lake of blood. I have always felt sorry for poor Tanga, and I fancy that he must have been very fat and always laughing in his high voice, and that having been brought up among women he missed that kind of life, and had to start something of the same sort where he would be still a servant helping women to lovers even when he had been made master.

"Towards the end of his life Boss Hardy became jealous of everyone, as if he were mad. First he tried to kill his brother-in-law Shampoo, who, warned by his sister, ran off to the Whydahs, who made him their general. Then the king became jealous of the old Gaw who had served him faithfully all his life, and who had saved him a hundred times from the consequences of his own cowardice and folly. Boss Hardy had his general tied up, and taking a cutlass began to cut his head off in front of the palace in the great square of Abomey. But when he had finished his speech to the troops, his heart failed him, for he was afraid. He struck the Gaw one blow with a shaking hand, then he threw down the cutlass, and began screaming, while the old man, with his head half cut off, lay looking at his master without making a sound, and it is said smiling, though his face was all over blood. At last Boss Hardy gave the order for the Gaw to be strangled."

"That's beastly," said Francis. "What happened to the brute in the end? I hope he was murdered."

"Oh no indeed," said Tulip. "After that he sent an army against the Whydahs, but Shampoo retreated before it and drew it on into the lagoons, and there set on it, killing all but twenty-four men, whom he sent back to the king with insulting messages. Their fate was worse than those that died in battle, for Boss Hardy put them all to death with his own hand as an example to his soldiers, so that they should learn never to be defeated. Ten years after that the Whydahs again attacked Whydah, but there happening to be a very brave Englishman called Ajangan in the town, they could not capture it. Boss Hardy died when he was seventy years old, and there was great rejoicing. He was my great-great-grandfather. I hope you do not think that I am like him. I have told you that story," Tulip went on, "so that you should understand what sort of people we are; cruel, savage, and liking the sight of blood. Here in England you never do cruel things like those I have been telling you about. There are no people like my great-great-grandfather here;

only good people. All the same I think we laugh more and have more fun than you do." And saying this Tulip laughed herself, pinched Francis in the arm, and then picking up their baskets of mushrooms they set out for home. On the way Sambo suddenly looked at Francis with a sly smile very different from his usual grin, pointed to his clenched fist and nodded. When his uncle bent down to him he opened his fingers; stuck to his moist brown palm were the speckled wings of a little blue butterfly.

When Francis and Tulip came in sight of the inn they saw that the door was wide open, with a hurdle lying across the threshold, and William's coat beside it on the ground, then as they drew nearer the loud rumour of many voices came to their ears. There was no one in either of the bars, but looking further they found the kitchen and the scullery full of men, whilst in the orchard beyond, groups of labourers were standing under the apple trees. A silence fell when Tulip entered the kitchen, and in that moment she could hear the sound of heavy boots in the bedroom. She stood still then, threw up her hands, and without waiting to be told fled upstairs, and Sambo ran after her.

"The Governor's been fighting and has got hurt," said one of the men to Francis. "They have taken him upstairs," and suddenly Francis saw that in the scullery two men were holding a limp figure in a chair from which he would have slid, and that this figure was spitting blood. The boy went forward to see better; there was a basin of blood, a bucket of water, and several bloodstained cloths. "That is the fellow who did it, He'll swing for it if the Governor dies," "Coo how his ear does bleed," said the onlookers grinning foolishly. It was Jack Sait of Portsmouth, occasionally he made noises, asking for something, but no words could be distinguished. Francis turned back and found Tom Madgwick coming down the stairs. "How did this happen?" he asked.

"I was in the cellar," answered Tom. "I don't know how it started. I was bottling sherry. When I came up I saw Freddy Leake come in at the door. He asked me for a bucket of water and said the Captain was out in the orchard giving a fearful hiding to a fellow that had come along with Mr. Molten and his carter from Tarrant, and that they had fought two rounds already."

"We filled the bucket, and then went out into the orchard, and for the first minute we couldn't see anyone there because of the little dip in the ground. When we had got close up to him we saw Captain Targett lying as if he were dead, and that chap there sitting under a tree all over blood. There has been foul play somewhere." Then Tom turned to the men in the kitchen and shouted angrily: "Now then you get out of here," and pointed to the door. "A lot of dirty cowards," he cried as they moved out of the room leaving only the old blacksmith Burden and his mate Freddy Leake, who were holding up the drooping figure of the boxer. "There's been foul play, and not one of them will own to seeing anything, but I saw them poking their heads over the hedge. There will be some questions for them to answer." Then Tom turned to the smith. "That chap must be taken in to the police," he said.

"That's all right mate," answered Fred; "we won't let him go."

Just at that moment there was the sound of a woman's skirts rustling, and Tulip appeared in the doorway. Her eyeballs rolled; the flashing whites were the only movement in her black and stolid face; her hands were folded in front of her.

"Have you sent for the doctor?" she asked, and almost as soon as she had spoken, without waiting for an answer, she went out of the room.

At her words all the men started guiltily; no one had thought of the doctor.

"I'll ride over and fetch him," said Francis, who wanted to do something. "Where does he live?" And while the blacksmith began to give directions Tom ran to saddle the pony.

As Francis went out he met Tulip coming down the stairs again. "Tell the doctor that William's skull is broken," she said. "I can feel the edges of the bone."

"How is he?" asked Francis.

"I think that they have killed him," she answered simply, and at these words the boy ran out, jumped on his pony before Tom had fixed the girths, and a moment afterwards was galloping out of the village. When he had seen the doctor, who promised to come at once, Francis returned to the inn, where he found Freddy Leake, who had dropped in to talk over the fight with Tom and have a pint of beer. It was already dark, and the bar was lit by candles instead of the usual lamp.

"Well, the first thing I saw," said Freddy, "were a lot of the chaps going up the lane, but I thought nothing of that at the time. Then I stepped up here to the bar to have a glass of beer, for the forge makes me thirsty in this weather, not that I'm a drinking man."

At these words Tom gave Francis a wink and the blacksmith took another pull at his tankard and went on:

"Mr. Targett was here and drew me my glass, and then I said I must be getting along, for there was a horse waiting for his shoes. Mr. Targett stepped out into the road with me, and just then Mr. Molten came up with his carter and that fellow there, and Mr. Molten said something about a whip. You know what an easy way Mr. Targett has of chaffing. Well he began like that with the carter; he told him he must be careful about running or he would strain his heart; I can tell you it made me laugh to hear him. Carter did not like that and said: 'That black girl of yours is too saucy for our liking, Mr. Targett, and you set her up in it by dressing her as if she were a lady. What she wants is a touch of a whip like mine. You can have it if you will promise to use it, but if you don't I shall use it on her myself the first time that ever I see her. It's my whip and we have come to take it, if we have to use force.' Mr. Targett hit him then, and swore he would give a thrashing he would remember, but this other fellow they call Jack. . ."

"Sait his name is," said Tom. "He's an old prize-fighter, that has been known a long time at Portsmouth."

"Well he pushed in between them, and told Mr. Targett to take him on if he wanted a fight, and then Mr. Molten said: 'We have brought him along on purpose; you won't ride over him in a hurry.' I could see that something was coming then you understand, so I let them wait for me down at the forge. Mr. Targett pulled his coat off, but the Portsmouth fellow suggested going somewhere quieter, and we all went round the end of the house into the orchard."

"Sait his name is," said Tom for the second time. "I have seen him several times at Portsmouth and Gosport hanging round the public-houses in company with sailors; he's a known man there, but getting too old for his business."

"Well then they started," said the smith. Mr. Targett is the taller, and a bit longer in the reach, but the other fellow is a strong enough chap too. Mr. Targett held him off all the time, and kept slipping and ducking and jumping back out of his reach, and for the first minute Sait was chasing him round and round in a circle. But he never hit Mr. Targett, that is there was no blow to speak of. Presently Mr. Targett seemed to think that he had gone far enough, for he stood his ground toe to toe with him, and then didn't he leather him! That was when the blood began to fly, for every second or two Mr. Targett would catch him on that swollen ear of his. Mr. Molten and his carter hadn't anything to say then, for they had been calling out to Sait when he looked like winning. The fight was all one way after that, and I think myself that the reason was that Mr. Targett was too quick for him. He always seemed to get away from Sait's blows; he kept stopping them with his elbows, and dodging them." And the smith got up, stuck out his elbows, bobbed his head and gave a tremendous blow in the empty air.

"Several times the other fellow got hold of him, but Mr. Targett shook him off and then started hammering him again, and never let his ear alone. At last Sait got both his arms round him, and hugged him, and I could see Mr. Targett laughing in his face, and he caught him a right-handed round-arm blow on his ear as they went down together with the Portsmouth chap on top."

"Well that was round number one," said Tom. "What happened after that?"

"Well as soon as they got up Mr. Molten started swearing at Sait. 'Jack,' he said, 'you damned liar, you have made a fool of me in front of all the fellows here, and taken a sovereign of mine too. If I ever see you round my farm again I'll let daylight into you!' and with that he climbed over the hedge and we could hear him cursing the fellows in the lane, and telling them to get back to their work. I thought Mr. Targett would have hurt himself then with laughing. He said to the fellow: 'I reckon you have *earned* your sovereign; *earned* it old man; now shall we go and have a drink, mate, to the big surprise that's coming in the ring?' but Sait would not agree to that. 'I'll fight to a finish,' he said, 'the same as I always do. Maybe in another hour's time I shall stop you of laughing.'

"In the second round it was the same thing over again, only it lasted longer, and Mr. Targett knocked Sait off his feet once, but he got up again and they went on. The end of that round was just the same as the first one, Mr. Targett laughing at the fellow, and fibbing him on the ear while Sait hugged him and threw him. It was only then that you could see the other fellow's strength. Well that was all I saw. When Mr. Targett got up there wasn't a mark on him beyond a cut lip, and Sait lay there streaming with blood. The carter was bending over him, and then Mr. Targett said to me: 'Freddy,' he said, 'run and get some water for him, there's a good fellow. Fetch a bucketfull.' Those were the last words I heard Mr. Targett say."

"There must have been foul play while your back was turned," said Tom.

"They were two to one!" cried Francis.

"And there was no sign of that carter when we came out with the bucket," said Tom.

"Well, we know what Sait said down at the smithy, before they drove him in to Dorchester." said Freddy Leake, emptying his tankard.

"What is his story?" asked Francis.

"Just half a pint more Tom," said the smith. "Why his story is this: he says that after I went they started fighting again, and that Mr. Targett hit him a blow between the eyes that half stunned him, and then took hold of him and threw him, and fell with him, and that is all he knows about it."

"You won't get me to believe that," said Tom scornfully.

"Why not?" asked Francis, "that may be the truth, for if William was on the ground the carter might have kicked him."

"Aye that he might," said Freddy. "Another half a pint Tom."

"Yes, but if carter kicked him," said Tom drawing the beer, "Jack Sait saw him do it, and if he won't tell on him it is because it was as much his doing as carter's."

The door opened and the doctor entered.

"This way Sir," said Tom, and taking a candle he showed him down the passage and up the stairs. He did not come back.

Francis could hear the doctor's footsteps in the room overhead, and then the sound of some question addressed to Tulip. There was no answer, only the sound of footsteps on the plank floor, and the splash of water being poured into a basin.

"Coo—You ought to have seen your brother jabbing him on his great ear," said Freddy. Francis did not reply, he shivered, listening to what was going on in the room above where the doctor's voice sounded like the rapid snipping of scissors. When this sound stopped there were a few words from Tulip, spoken clearly and sufficiently loud for the boy to hear. "I understand. . . I have seen this before. . . I understand. . ."

The doctor came downstairs and without saying a word went out of the house. There was the noise of the wheels of his gig as he turned his horse round, and then the trot of his horse going away.

"Coo—your brother is a heavy man to handle," said the blacksmith. "Tom and I had a job with him on the stairs."

The boy sat silent for another five minutes till the door opened softly and Mrs. Clall put her head into the bar. "Doctor says he cannot last through the night," she said. The parrot scraped in its cage. "Time, gentlemen, please. Time," it said feebly.

"I thought he would be taken," said Freddy. Then he added: "Tell Tom I shall want another half-pint before he shuts up."

Francis picked up the candle and went out to the stable. The air was warm and still and the flame did not flicker out of doors. While he saddled his pony Francis began to cry, and in his pain first kissed the shaggy face of the little cob, and then struck the animal several times with his clenched fist. As he rode away he saw Tulip's shadow black against the curtain. When he had been riding half an hour he dismounted to cut a stick from a hedge, and after that he thrashed the pony unmercifully as he rode. Before midday William's elder brother, John Targett, drove up to the inn with Francis beside him. They were met by Tom, who told them that William had died in the night, and showed them up to the bedroom where Tulip was still sitting. When they entered she was talking rapidly in a low voice in English, but neither of them could distinguish the words, and so they could not know that she was addressing William's spirit, which she believed was there in the room with her, unaltered by death, and having the same desires as before it left the body.

John Targett gazed for a few moments at the face of his younger brother, while Francis tried to conceal his emotion by speaking to Sambo. But when Tulip said to them that Tom would give them each a glass of wine, he burst into tears, and left the room.

John Targett was very like William in the face, only a trifle more burly and not so tall, so that Tulip knew at once who he was and felt at home with him.

"A terrible end," he said. "All of our family seem to come by death violently. This is a shocking affair, and for no one more than you. I cannot forgive myself for not coming to see William; there are so many things to attend to everyday, and suddenly death separates us. I meant to come at the wedding. I sent a cheese but they never gave it to William; he would have liked to have tasted our cheese again. Well now I suppose there is a great deal of business to be done, and I had better undertake to deal with it."

John went downstairs, and without beating about the bush told Tom to hand over the keys and any money in his charge, and to put up the shutters and lock the door, which had not been done. The same evening, John visited the undertaker and the clergyman, and the next morning drove in to Dorchester to see the coroner. It appeared after a rough valuation of the effects at the inn that all the debts left by the dead man could be discharged, and that after this had been done there would be a sum of twenty or thirty pounds for the widow.

After William's death Tulip sat motionless in the room with the corpse. The blinds were drawn, and the windows shut. Sometimes she spoke in a low voice, and what was strange, always in English, but often she was silent for hours at a time, and motionless also, but at last she was driven out by the coroner's man and the undertaker.

On the morning of the funeral several parties arrived at "The Sailor's Return." In one dogcart came Mrs. John Targett and her nephew, Charlie Tizard, who went out into the orchard to smoke a pipe. In the next came Dolly and her husband (for she had been married now a few weeks). Then in a third dogcart came Lucy and Mr. Sturmey. Tulip had dressed herself that day in a black dress, over her head she wore a black lace shawl which concealed almost all her face, and she wore also the black gloves Dolly had given her.

When she went downstairs she found the company assembled, waiting to start for the churchyard. There was a sound of the men moving to and fro in the next room with the coffin, and carrying it out to the hearse, which had been hired from Wareham. Dolly kissed Sambo, and took Tulip in her arms, then she introduced her husband who shook hands. Stevie Barnes was a thin young man with a nutcracker nose and jaw, and was ill at ease, being the only person not attired in full mourning. Mr. Sturmey also came up to Tulip and said it was very extraordinary they had not met before. Then he smiled at her and nodded encouragement, though Tulip did not notice this. Her face was calm. She was entirely occupied in the effort of following correctly a foreign ritual, and behaving as she knew William would have wished her to behave. She was stiff and silent, for she knew that any breach of decorum would be a bad omen. The whole village of Maiden Newbarrow attended the funeral, and many others who had known William had come in from the neighbouring parishes. This was not only due to the fact that he had been generally respected, but also that he had become notable by the manner of his death. Those who most regretted that they had not seen him get his injuries, now thought they would make up in some degree by coming to see him buried.

All the Targett family had brought wreaths, and in addition there was one sent by Mr. Stingo, and another from old Mr. Estrich.

After the service Dolly walked back with Tulip, and the whole company sat down to dinner.

John carved and said grace. In the conversation which followed, William and the existence of Tulip and Sambo were ignored, for Dolly was now separated from Tulip, who sat at the bottom of the table with Sambo between Francis and Charlie Tizard and they were silent throughout the meal.

When dinner was over they went into the adjoining room, where John addressed the assembled family. William, he said, was his brother, and he, as the head of the family, had to perform the duty of looking into his affairs. In the last year William had run through a small fortune, and now there was nothing to show for it. Fortunately there was enough to cover the debts, and after disposing of the inn there would be a small balance for his widow, which would enable her to look about her. Mr. Stingo had met him in a generous spirit, and had relieved them of the tenancy of the inn. He himself was going to put up a headstone to William and would pay for it out of his own pocket, as he felt that he ought not to be forgotten.

"What will happen to the child?" asked Dolly, when her brother had finished speaking; "we must remember that he is our nephew."

"I don't think we have much reason to call that little black boy a relative of ours," said Lucy.

There was a moment's silence, then John said: "I have spoken to Mr. Cronk about the child. Lucy you can also keep an eye on them for the present; and now I am going to give Mrs. William a sum of money to go on with."

"How long can she stay here?" asked Dolly.

"The sale is next week, and she had better move out at once."

"There is no reason she should stay here that I can see," said Dolly. "Couldn't she come home with us?" And she turned to her husband.

"Do what you think right about it Dolly," said Stevie.

But when the question was put to her, Tulip shook her head.

"I'm all right," she said, "I have Sambo."

"I do not know that she is a fit person to have the child," said Lucy. "We can't foster a heathen."

"I have asked Mr. Cronk to decide what should be done about the child, and he is writing to some friends of his. We can safely leave the question in his hands," said John. "For the present the child is to stay with her."

"She is a most unsuitable person to be given money. I think it ought to be given to someone who can be relied on," said Lucy.

"William would not like you to have his money," said Tulip.

There was a silence, then Francis laughed.

"Give it to Tulip," said Dolly, "it belongs to her."

"What Dolly says is quite right," answered John. "I have no legal right to give the money to anyone but Mrs. William, and I shall do best to stick to the law."

He rose, looked at his watch, and said: "It is blowing up for rain; we had better be moving."

They all got up, scraping their chairs.

"Well Mrs. William, here is the money. I have no doubt William would have given it to you himself," and he took out a small canvas bag as he spoke.

"Here are fifteen pounds, which is the money from the sale of everything except the furniture. I have sold the linen and plate and most of the bedroom furniture, privately. Things never fetch much at a sale. I reckon there should be another ten pounds coming to you later on, but I shall see to it that a proper provision is made for you."

The members of the Targett family dispersed. Outside their traps were waiting; Tom had been harnessing the horses.

At parting Dolly kissed Tulip, and Francis gave her sixpence to buy sweets for Sambo.

Lucy and her husband drove away silently, for Lucy considered that she had been insulted, and that John had shown himself weak and hesitating as ever.

That night Tulip was left alone, and she sat up late packing her things. First she took down all her dresses and her clothes and spread them on the bed, and on the table, and the chest of drawers. She stayed for a long while fingering the silks and satins, and then began to fold them up, and burst into a flood of tears. She carried them in her arms downstairs, opened the kitchen door and went out into the orchard; afterwards she brought paper, several armfuls of straw, and a faggot from the woodpile.

She set light to her bonfire, and when it was ablaze she threw all the finery William had given her upon the flames. One by one she threw the garments, first a silk shawl, then a pair of silk stockings, and then an embroidered gown. While she was employed in this fashion Tom, who had been woken by the light shining in his window, looked out.

"Whatever are you doing there Mrs. Tulip?" he asked her.

But Tulip did not answer, and by the light of the flaming faggots he could see what she was about. He was ashamed then to say anymore to her, though his good sense was shocked by the destruction of so many fine things, several of which she had worn but once, when William had first brought them home to her.

When she had finished burning her fine clothes, not sparing one thing, and leaving herself nothing but the clothes she wore ordinarily in the kitchen, she smeared her head in the ashes, singeing her woolly crop of hair. She went indoors after that and left the last flames to die away by themselves. Just then the first heavy drops of the storm of rain, which John had foretold, fell like a shower of stones.

Next day Tom was up early, for he was going that morning back to his home at Cowes. When he had had his breakfast he knocked at the door of her room and Tulip opened it; she had not undressed that night, nor for that matter had she slept. "I am just come to say good-bye Mrs. Tulip, to you and to Sambo," said Tom.

"Where are you going then Tom?" asked she.

"Well I must be going to my home, and then looking out for a new place you know," said Tom. "I must say good-bye now or I shall not get to Southampton tonight."

"Why, take me with you," said Tulip. "I am going to Southampton myself. I shall not stay here, or they will make me give up Sambo. The parson is to steal Sambo. William never wanted his son to be a parson; he was to be a harpooneer."

"Yes I have heard him say so often," answered Tom. "Come along then with me, Mrs. Tulip, if you want to go to Southampton. I shall be near home there and will soon find you lodgings; you know my home is at Cowes, and we are always going to and fro to Southampton, and I have great acquaintance in that town."

Tulip had only a little bundle with her, and was soon ready. The carrier was waiting outside for Tom to take him to the station, for he had a chest with him, and Tulip and Sambo drove off without anyone taking any notice of them. But even when she got to Southampton, where Tom found her very respectable lodgings, Tulip did not fancy she was clear of the clergyman. She had learnt that distance meant very little to the superior white people who had money. She made then all haste to get a ship to take herself and Sambo out of England, one that was bound for the coast of Guinea, and that would set her down within five or six hundred miles of her father's kingdom. She was a long time enquiring at the docks, but fruitlessly. Either there was no ship in the port bound that way, or else the sailors would not listen to her but only answered her very lewdly. Thus Tulip spent two months in the town without finding the ship she wanted. Every week she had to pay the woman a pound for the room and for the food which she and Sambo ate.

One day after she had been seeking thus for a ship for over two months, she came in with Sambo to her lodging, and the woman who boarded them said to her:

"Why Mrs. Targett only this minute there was a clergyman here asking after you. He is but this moment gone; if you run up the street towards the Bar-gate, you will be sure to catch him."

Tulip did not wait longer but to secure her purse, and picking up Sambo, ran into the street, but then she did not run towards the Bar-gate, but the other way to the docks.

So she went running and hurrying down towards the harbour almost ready to get aboard the first ship she came to, and travel to any part of the world, for she was quite out of breath with fear. Just as she got to the docks she was hailed by a seaman.

"Hullo my lass," cried he, "you are the purchase I have been looking for. I'm tired of the gear in this country, and wish I were back at Whydah. Come on my girl, and give me some proper fun. I'll do your business for you."

Now what struck Tulip's ear was not his offering at her, for she had been plentifully pestered in this way all the time that she had been in Southampton, but that word "Whydah," which was just the place of all others which she aimed at reaching.

She stopped dead in her tracks, and went up to him and asked him gently: "Do you know Whydah then?"

"Why my lass, I have just come from Whydah, and we sail again tomorrow for the coast."

"Oh take me to your Captain then," said Tulip, "for Whydah is near to my home, and I want to find a ship to carry me there."

"Take you to the Captain," cried the sailor laughing. "Nay he's too old for such business, but I'll do your turn and give you half a crown for it."

"No sailor," said Tulip, but smiling for she would not offend the man if she could help it since he was her one hope. "I know you sailors, you'll find another girl easily. But please take me to your captain, for my husband was the captain of a trading vessel on the coast and was most likely a friend of his."

The fellow was then overcome by her beseeching and imploring him to take her to his captain, and though he would not do that he led her along to the house where the captain of his ship lodged, and then left her on the doorstep to try her luck. As it fell out the captain was just drinking a cup of tea and warming his feet at the fire, and he heard Tulip's voice when she asked for him. The woman who opened the door would have shut it in Tulip's face, for she hated a negro like the plague, but Tulip stuck her foot in the jamb, and kept her parleying.

"Tell the captain I am Mrs. Targett, and I am the widow of a friend of his." Now as it chanced what Tulip said thus in mere bravado was truth, and the captain had indeed known Targett, or at any rate heard speak of him often enough, and since he had got back to England had heard him spoken of again, with particulars of his death. He came then to the door with the teapot in his hand, and said that Tulip might come in, which she did instantly, holding Sambo by the hand. The captain eyed her up and down, and seeing that she was respectably dressed, though very plainly, asked her what service he could do her.

"Only give me a passage, with my little boy, to Whydah," said she. "I am the daughter of a great man in Dahomey, and now my husband, Captain Targett, is dead, and I want to go back to Africa. If I stay here, who knows what will become of my little Sambo. He will be treated as if he were a slave, he will be only a dirty nigger, but in Dahomey he will be a great man, and cousin of the heir to the throne."

"Well," said the captain, "I have never carried any passengers and I won't carry a woman on board my ship. It is a bad place enough as it is, but it would be hell if I had a woman aboard. But I will take your little boy if you like, for the sake of Captain Targett, whom I have often heard of, indeed I believe I met him."

Tulip began then to beg and beseech him to take her as well, and would have fawned on him and licked his boots, to see if that would move him. But the captain remained firm, and indeed told her not to say another word or he would not take the boy either. So that at last Tulip was forced to be silent, and stood turning the thing over in her mind.

But considering that the clergyman was waiting for her now at her lodgings, come to take Sambo from her and send him God knows where into what orphanage or asylum, and that then he would stay a dirty nigger all his life, and that she would lose him anyhow; thinking as I say of this, she nodded her head, and taking Sambo's hand put it silently into the captain's. For she could not speak for fear that she should start a-blubbering or a-moaning, and so offend.

"Well I'll take him on board right away," said the captain. "We sail tomorrow on the tide, and he shall sleep aboard the ship. The steward will look after him."

Then Tulip took out her purse and said: "This is all the money I have got, but I have more coming, ten or twelve pounds more, and I will pay it to you when you come back if this is not enough for a child's passage. And if there be any balance to spare pay it to my cousin the Prince Choodaton and commend Sambo to him."

The captain laughed at this and said he would not take her money, but afterwards he took it, saying:

"I will not charge you any passage money, but this will serve for me to hire bearers on Whydah beach to take your boy up-country. I shall see him safe into the hands of Choodaton. He is a man I have heard spoken of. Come along my lad, you shall come and see my ship and the sailors dancing on the deck."

So Tulip took farewell of her child, and not so tenderly either, as she might have done if the captain had not been there with his boots just laced up waiting to take Sambo on board. And all little Sambo thought of was to see the sailors dancing on the deck, for he did not know that he was to lose his mother.

When she had left them, Tulip wandered about for sometime like a demented thing. But at last some drunken sailors clutching at her set her off running, and she got a fair way out of the town on the west side, and lay down in a ditch and rested there that night. Next morning she would not go back to Southampton, lest the ship had not sailed and the clergyman should find her, so she wandered out into the country.

For some days she travelled about aimlessly, begging her food at cottages, and then she directed her steps to Dorset, since there was money waiting for her there.

When she got to Maiden Newbarrow it was late, past eleven o'clock at night, and she was very weary with walking. She went to the inn, and finding the doors locked, pushed in the catch of the kitchen window, and so got inside the house. She lay down then in an empty room and was soon asleep lying on the bare boards. When she awoke she heard someone moving, and the voices of a man and of a woman and before she could get onto her feet the door opened. In the doorway was the wife of the new tenant, for they were moving in that day and were expecting their furniture to come that morning.

"Why Fred, whatever's here?" she cried, then looking at Tulip's black face, she exclaimed: "I'll be bound it's the poor creature that ran away, Mr. Targett's wife."

Her husband then came into the room, and they questioned Tulip about what she had done, and where she had been, and told her that Jack Sait had been found guilty of murder two days since, and that he would be hanged in six weeks' time.

"A villain like that deserves no mercy," said the new landlord; "murdering a licensed man. You have a pleasure left to look forward to; for I warrant you will be glad to see the brute hanged."

"Why should I?" answered Tulip. "I have seen so many deaths, I do not care about them anymore."

While they were still talking, the waggon loaded with their furniture drove up, and the waggoners began to unload it. At first Tulip only watched the men moving to and fro, but presently she reflected that the new glasses must be rinsed, and the beds made, and that there was a great deal of work to be done on such a day, so she set to work with the others. Then she saw a new kettle and drew water from the well, and filled it, and after lighting the fire, she brewed a pot of tea and took it in to the new mistress. As Tulip's grace or beauty, if one can use such a word about a black negro woman, was now a good deal faded by her recent misfortunes, the inn-keeper's wife never thought of Tulip as likely to attract the men. And seeing the negress would make herself useful, she spoke to her husband about letting her stay on.

He was a good-natured enough man, and was fond of a joke, so he said: "Yes Minnie, she can do all the dirty work, and she won't show it, that's one thing. Yes, let her stay on and welcome; she can rinse out the glasses behind the bar, and she will cost us nothing for wages, or next to nothing. Yes, no one shall say I turned the poor creature out of doors now she has nowhere to go."

Thus Tulip went on living at the inn, working all day long as the drudge of everyone about the place. In the village they were used to her, and now that she was always dressed in the poorest cast-off clothes her mistress had given her, nobody shouted at her or jeered as she went by. But by degrees her name changed from Mrs. Tulip to Mrs. Two Lips, because as Tulip grew older and uglier her lips grew broader and more blubbery.

Three months after she had come back, Tulip sent the rest of her money to the Captain at Southampton, but she never got an answer or an acknowledgement from him, and not knowing how to get news of Sambo, had to live on without any.

Some ten years later John Targett was killed by a bull, and Harry came back on a visit to his native country, his business being to make over the farm to Francis, his younger brother. While he was in England he heard all the circumstances of William's death and that Tulip was living and still at "The Sailor's Return."

He did not visit her, although business took him to Maiden Newbarrow to see Lucy. Ten years in America had changed him. He had fought in the Southern army in the Civil War, he had learned to know the negro better than he did when he first met Tulip, and he would have said, better than his brother William ever could have done. Certainly he had made more money out of negroes than William had by selling poor Tulip's pearls, though not so pleasantly. Tulip heard of his visit to Lucy. She was not surprised, she was not even disappointed that he did not come to see her, for she had learned to know her station in life, and she did her duty in it very well.

A Note About the Author

David Garnett (1892–1981) was a British writer. Born in Brighton, East Sussex, Garnett was the son of Edward Garnett, a critic and publisher, and Constance Clara Black, a translator of Russian known for bringing the works of Chekhov and Dostoevsky to an English audience. A pacifist, he spent the years of the First World War as a conscientious objector working on fruit farms along the eastern coast England. As a member of the Bloomsbury Group, he befriended many of the leading artists and intellectuals of his day. After publishing his debut novel, *Dope-Darling* (1918), under a pseudonym, he won the James Tait Black Memorial Prize for *Lady into Fox* (1922), an allegorical fantasy novel. His 1955 novel *Aspects of Love* was adapted into a musical of the same name by Andrew Lloyd Webber. Alongside poet Francis Meynell, Garnett founded the Nonesuch Press, an independent publisher known for its editions of classic novels, poetry collections, and children's books. Garnett, a bisexual man, had relationships with fellow Bloomsbury Group members Francis Birrell and Duncan Grant, and was married twice in his life. Following the death of his first wife Ray, with whom he had two sons, Grant married Angelica Bell, the daughter of Grant and Vanessa Bell, whose sister was renowned novelist Virginia Woolf. Together, the Garnetts raised four daughters, three of whom went on to careers in the arts. Following his divorce from Angelica, Garnett spent the rest of his life in Montcuq, France.

A Note from the Publisher

Printed in the USA
CPSIA information can be obtained
at www.ICGtesting.com
JSHW080003150824
68134JS00021B/2259